THE NEGRO
GRANDSONS
OF
VERCINGETORIX

ALAIN MABANCKOU

THE NEGRO GRANDSONS OF VERCINGETORIX

TRANSLATED BY BILL JOHNSTON

INDIANA UNIVERSITY PRESS

This book is a publication of

Indiana University Press
Office of Scholarly Publishing
Herman B Wells Library 350
1320 East 10th Street
Bloomington, Indiana 47405 USA

iupress.indiana.edu

Original publication in French
© 2002 by Le serpent à plumes
English translation © 2019
by Bill Johnston

*Manufactured in the United
States of America*

Cataloging information is available
from the Library of Congress.

ISBN 978-0-253-04388-7 (paperback)
ISBN 978-0-253-04385-6 (ebook)

1 2 3 4 5   23 22 21 20 19

To my mother Pauline Kengué
To Henri Lopes
For Khadi Hane

NOTE FROM THE FRENCH PUBLISHER

We recently received a notebook entitled *The Negro Grandsons of Vercingetorix*. Our editorial board made the decision to publish it. The text is signed by a certain Hortense Iloki.

According to Léopold Mpassi-Mpassi, who submitted the manuscript to us and who resides in France, at present the author is supposedly somewhere in the forests of southern Vietongo.

A separate sheet of paper, serving as a preface to the account, indicates that Hortense Iloki wished the reader to know something about her country from the beginning, before learning the facts that she relates. We include this note by way of introduction:

> A former French colony in central Africa, the Republic of Vietongo numbers more than 2.6 million inhabitants and covers an area of 342,000 square kilometers. Its people, the Vietongolese, are mostly concentrated in large urban areas, including Mapapouville, the political capital, and Pointe-Rouge, the financial capital. The literacy rate is one of the highest in French-speaking Africa. Mapapouville was previously the capital of French Equatorial Africa (FEA) and of Free France under General de Gaulle.

The country is inhabited by several different ethnic groups; political power is held by the Northerners, a minority population. The economy is reliant on oil, which brings in about 90 percent of state revenue. This wealth, however, has not resulted in viable economic development.

Since 1958 Vietongo's mosaic of ethnicities has been a source of friction orchestrated by political figures.

The current head of state is General Edou. He previously ruled for thirteen years, then was defeated by His Excellency Lebou Kabouya in the first democratic elections held in our country. It was the first time someone from the South had led Vietongo. General Edou went into exile in Europe during the five years of his southern rival's term of office. He returned to power after driving out His Excellency Lebou Kabouya . . .

* * *

By the time people read this notebook, I may no longer be of this world.

My name is Hortense Iloki, and I am a northerner. I ought not to have had any reason to worry, really, since on that day my people, meaning those of my ethnic group, had come to power. But things are not so simple as that.

I had married Kimbembé, a southerner who was a native of the same region as Vercingetorix and His Excellency Lebou Kabouya, two characters the reader will meet very soon. The facts I relate here concern what without any doubt has been the darkest period of our country's history. I've also included details from my own life and those of the people around me. But does my life not resemble the lives of all Vietongolese?

FOREWORD TO THE NOTEBOOK

I have to exercise patience in order to speak objectively of what has been happening to us.

Ever since I was a young teenager in the North of the country, I've always written regularly in composition books. I can't explain this constant penchant for confession. Today I'm motivated more by the fear that the truth will one day be obliterated. I've lost count of how many pages I've amassed, and especially of the number of times I've reread them. By now I know them by heart, to the point that I sometimes recite them unawares, like an old tune from who knows where that I carry within myself, humming it all day long...

Since the course of events has led us to think something is likely to happen to us soon, I've decided to retrace in this notebook all that I had previously noted here and there without any concern for chronology. I may also be doing it because I'm convinced that my memory won't be able much longer to hold on to the facts, which grow more tangled with every day, or else that time, slowly donning its dark veil, will end up weaving a shroud of oblivion over these far-off events that today have disrupted our lives and those of the inhabitants of Vietongo, who for the most part are widely dispersed in the remote forests of the back country.

* * *

How long ago it was—that time when my youthful notebooks, which by the way I no longer have, described nothing more than my first romantic problems or the frustrations of a middle school student going through the onset of puberty. Depending on my mood, in one place I would draw hearts colored in pink and elsewhere others pierced by sharp arrows. In those days I was hard on those in my circle, describing them in every exaggerated detail. The least trifle was set down, including comments in the margin, often with caricatures of people who annoyed me. Like other girls my age, I cultivated the idea that my parents and the little society of adults in our district were getting in the way of my independence. The notebooks were my refuge, a safe place where I could reveal myself without embarrassment.

I remember I also wrote poems. Many years later I found this poetry laughable and of no interest, and I didn't even dare look back at my confessional pages in the light of day. It was obvious I didn't have a poetic bone in my body. What I had taken for poetry was in reality nothing more than a series of lamentations and alarmingly mawkish declarations of love. Anger, jealousy, and resentment prevailed over any notion of creativity.

I don't regret that experience. It helped me learn that everything I felt, saw, or heard ought to be noted down somewhere. I felt so frail, so vulnerable, that for me it was the only way to face up to reality, to converse with invisible characters who took the time to listen to me, put themselves in my place, understand my state of mind before offering me advice.

Kimbembé, my husband, the man we've left, used to make fun of my writings, especially during the first years we knew each other in the North of the country, my native region . . .

* * *

I'm sometimes angry with myself about it.

Then remorse comes flooding in. A wave, a swell that's hard to hold back. I yield to a surge of guilt that passes through my soul like an electric shock and paralyzes my left hand, the same one that acts as my go-between in recalling and writing down the facts.

All at once, frozen in place, I don't write another word more, my memory unsettled through and through, my thoughts piecemeal and disordered. At moments like that I close my eyes and try to empty my burning head. Voices that are distant yet so very familiar murmur scarcely audible words. I revisit the past one more time: the time when things began, the moment they got worse, the way the Vietongolese were so stunned. Angry faces, changed over time, loom like apocalyptic shades: Christiane Kengué, Gaston Okemba, Kimbembé, General Edou, His Excellency Lebou Kabouya, Vercingetorix, his Negro Grandsons, the Anacondas, the Romans, and many other characters . . .

THE NEGRO GRANDSONS
OF
VERCINGETORIX

PART ONE
FAREWELL TO CHRISTIANE

I

Mam'Soko and Her Cane

Mam'Soko, the owner of the house we're staying in here, often comes by. She lives over there, opposite us. She passes round the back, through the bamboo, by Crayfish Creek. With amazing energy for her age, and despite the sickness that's eating her away, she uses her cane to clear twigs and dead leaves out of her path. She talks to herself, mumbles forgotten songs, spits on the ground, and utters insults in a dialect we do not understand. We're not the ones she abuses in this way, as we initially thought.

Some days Mam'Soko strolls about in her orchard. She picks up fruit that has fallen in the night. Mangoes, papayas, soursops, figs. She gathers them up, sits beneath a tree, and eats them. The juice trickles from her mouth. She licks her fingers, chases away the flies. When she's eaten her fill, she leans back against the tree and dozes, lulled by the singing of the cicadas. She snores, traveling little by little toward other skies. She doesn't leave the orchard till it's very late and the sun, transformed into a tiny rust-red disk, is taking shelter behind the hills, shining only weakly. At that point Mam'Soko climbs back up toward her house. Stooping, she holds her wrap dress with one hand as she walks. She lingers in front of an old mango tree in the middle of the orchard. Here she indulges in an act of love: she touches the bark of the tree tenderly. The tree exults, responds to her caress, shakes its leaves. Mam'Soko draws close to the trunk, sniffs at it as if to recall the time she planted it. It was one of the first trees in the orchard. How could she remember the year when she'd buried a nut in the ground? Between her and the tree, time has become irrelevant. The tree is there; that's all there is to it. Mam'Soko recognizes that, like her, the tree has also grown old. Intertwined wrinkles compete over its trunk. Its roots rise up out of the earth and perish in the sun. Its leaves are covered with a whitish coating. For sure this is gray hair.

She leaves her tree regretfully and heads toward the henhouse. She peers through the wire netting at the empty cubicles, the half-pecked scraps of root vegetables, the caked droppings, the eggshells. How many chickens and roosters are still alive in there? She's given up counting. Her poultry runs free in the village. "Old roosters see the dawn above the trees," say the elders.

As for her livestock, Mam'Soko has no idea where they are. There's nothing to indicate that the sheep and goats grazing in her orchard or behind her house belong to her. Only a few creatures have remained loyal to her. When they see her coming through the door, they go up to her, surround her, then follow her in single file to the orchard. This is the only way the old lady has of telling her animals from those of the other villagers. Mam'Soko talks to them. She asks them not to stray too far from her land . . .

Chronic Rheumatism

When she's done walking in the orchard, Mam'Soko goes back into her house. Ever since we've been here, she leaves the door half open. She doesn't want to go to bed right away. She's delaying that moment. She's mindful of the fact that lying down means delivering yourself to death. So she doesn't do so just yet. She takes a handful of tobacco leaves, folds them over and over, cuts them into little pieces, and chews them, sitting on her pallet. She closes her eyes, feels toughened, strengthened. Now she's capable of resisting, confronting the shadows of night that have fallen on the village. Her slack muscles suddenly tense up. Her nostrils flutter. Her heart strains, like a motor spinning in the mud. She's prepared her food as she's chewed the tobacco leaves. She feels stronger than the night and able to face up to it. Above all she mustn't light the hurricane lamp. She takes some ash from her hearth and puts it in a terra-cotta bowl. She adds water from Crayfish Creek. She stirs the mixture till it becomes a thick paste. She puts this medication on her joints. Once that's done she can sleep peacefully. This is how she combats chronic rheumatism, the illness that has twisted her fingers and toes. An illness that has dwelled in her for twenty years.

When the attacks come, she thinks about the end. She tells herself she won't make it through. That she ought to submit, place her knees on the ground, and resign herself to fate. She senses the ache beginning in her feet, tightening her stomach, and rising as far as her chest. She rears up on her pallet, holds her breath. She drinks a tumbler of lukewarm water. And she waits. Anything could come: the end, or remission. But she waits. And the pain passes, like a dark cloud displaced by the appearance of the sun. Now she can breathe again. She studies her fingers and toes. She takes some tobacco leaves, chews them greedily.

At the end of every attack, she tries to reset her toes and fingers. She gives them a less curled-up shape. She kneads them, strokes them, massages them, blows on them. Ash. Water. She spreads it on her fingers, her toes, her ankles, knees, elbows. The mixture brings a feeling of well-being ...

The Nighttime Visitor

Sometimes Mam'Soko bursts out laughing as she lists names that are unknown to us. And she doesn't stop. She comes into our house, sits down right on the ground. She rolls tobacco leaves, which she places between the stumps of her teeth. She has a special way of softening the leaves before chewing them. First she smells them, as a way of whetting her desire. Then she opens them out and rubs them between her palms. Finally she cuts them up with a penknife and savors them for a long time, like a ruminant.

Mam'Soko calls us by names other than our own. She is conjuring up the life of a man who, she says, is still alive, even though he was buried several decades ago near Crayfish Creek. And we learn that the man, whose name was Massengo, was her husband. That he was also the chief of this village. That he should be spoken of in the present tense. Mam'Soko swears he isn't dead. That we can see him every evening at her place when they eat together, in the shadows.

Her husband could not have been buried in a cemetery, the old woman tells us. He loathed those places. You can't relax in a cemetery. There's too much noise. The noise of the crows. The noise of the vultures. The noise of the widows and the orphans. The noise of the gravediggers. The noise of the domestic animals grazing nearby. No, her husband was much more likely to be somewhere restful. Where time stops. Where there's only one day. Where the meadows remain green. Where the seasons come to quench their thirst. That's where her husband rests. But, contradicting herself somewhat, no doubt because she no longer distinguishes the real world from the other one, later on she tells us the circumstances of Massengo's death.

We always listen to her without interrupting. We nod. We've grown used to her presence, her comings and goings. It comforts us to see her walking. We like her expression, on the mornings when she comes to tell us what she and her late husband have been saying to one another. Apparently she's told him about our being there. According to her, they spent one whole night talking about it, and her husband would be delighted to make our acquaintance.

The Open Door

On the days when Mam'Soko's door remains closed, we're immediately alarmed. First of all because we've grown used to seeing it half open. In addition, at her age, as she herself reminds us, death pays a visit every dawn. Mam'Soko describes death as a short, ageless woman dressed in rags, her face lowered, walking lopsidedly. She's decided that she's not going to be intimidated by some little woman coming to see her. It's because of that that she dreads closing her eyes and sleeping. She thinks that sleep draws on her face the expression she'll have on the day of her death. She says that sleeping is dying a little bit; it's practice so you'll be better at acting out the scene when the fateful day comes.

Mam'Soko's House

When she wants to talk to us, Mam'Soko taps on the window with her cane, and I go and open the door for her. She smiles at me. Her wrinkles crease up. Her wrap dress no longer hides her scrawny legs.

I think that in recent days, wandering in the orchard and around the house where we've taken shelter has given her a way to occupy herself. She comes by four or five times in the course of the day. When she finally goes back home, she only half closes her door, and we know she's watching us from behind it.

She's often said to us that she doesn't like light. In the shadows she nimbly avoids treading on the objects lying about on the floor: big cooking pots, aluminum lids, terra-cotta water jars, jugs, wooden spoons, bamboo drinking cups. In her house, even in this disorder each thing is where it belongs. Nothing has been left by accident. She knows where everything is. It only looks messy. Not one object is out of place. Except perhaps the bowl in which she makes her ash balm. And the bamboo cup she drinks from to stay hydrated on days when the fever is intense. She's thought of everything: she needs to be able to grab the bowl without getting up from her pallet.

Despite this disorder, the interior of her home is sparse. It's permanently humid in there, no doubt because of the lack of light, since the old lady keeps her windows closed. A basket hangs on the wall, recalling the years when she worked the earth. She made it herself almost half a century ago. Two ancient shotguns hang from a window frame: the shadow of her husband, who was regarded as the best hunter in the village. Mam'Soko's tobacco leaves lie on a low shelf near her bed. These too she can reach without getting up.

When we open the door to her, Mam'Soko looks at me for a moment, then turns her feeble eyes on my daughter, Maribé. She tells us that there's no point in staying cooped up like this, that we ought to get out and take a walk in the village. I reply that we prefer to rest up a little. The truth is that, in spite of my explanations, she hasn't grasped our reasons for being here.

Exhaustion

In order to make it all the way here to Louboulou, we had to set off into the remote bushlands of the South, come what may. During this trek, which took an entire day, when I realized my daughter was ready to drop, I put my hand on her shoulder and whispered words of encouragement. I don't remember exactly what I said that kept her going for such a long time. Maybe I promised her that we only had a few more kilometers to go, that once we'd skirted the hills looming in front of us, we'd find ourselves at the village my friend Christiane Kengué had spoken of the last time I saw her.

Did Maribé believe me?

It was a big lie, because as soon as we'd passed the heights that were by turns sheer or rounded, we could see other hills extending into the distance, ever steeper, covered with dense, jumbled vegetation. Maribé's stare revealed her incredulity. I can still see her dismay. Deep down, kilometer after kilometer, the journey was slowly sapping her strength.

On that day the sun had made its appearance earlier than usual, unleashing all its scorching heat from early morning. The air seemed captive, immobilized at the level of our nostrils. Even the most restless reptiles of the forest lazed in a circle in the shade of the trees. With a vexed expression, they eyed the unseen flames of the raging star that was consuming the dead leaves through a kind of calefaction. We could hear the grass groaning, then wilting in the space of a few minutes. The tiniest spark, a light tap of flint against flint, would have been enough for it to catch fire.

Maribé kept moving forward.

Sweat beaded her forehead. Her lips were dry. I quickly covered her head with an old wrap dress, one of those crimson ones worn by members of the Revolutionary Union of the Women of Vietongo, stamped with an effigy of General Edou. And we walked ahead resolutely, eyes fixed on the horizon, in hopes of seeing the first houses of Louboulou as we emerged from the forest.

But we were still walking.

In front of us, stretching into infinity was a savanna reduced to ashes: lantana bushes, fields of root vegetables or corn, banana plantations being ransacked by hordes of excited chimpanzees, which we came upon as they squabbled in the foliage overhead.

Maribé, borne along on bowed legs that were proving less and less stable, thought about taking off her rubber sandals, which, she claimed, were slowing her down. She gave up the idea, though, because as we plunged into the heart of the bush, we found that the ground was cracked and was becoming difficult, gravelly and thorny. All the same, she wanted to show me that she had strength in abundance, that she was capable of enduring more than one day of walking amid this vegetation, the tops of whose countless species brushed against the clouds.

Putting the Point of Departure out of Mind

It was at this moment that, at the far end of a large clearing lined with Palmyra palms, limbas, filao trees, okoumés, and bamboo, we spotted a river snaking amid shoals of pebbles. It cut through a gully before transforming into a deep, verdant carpet of algae, ferns, and water lilies. It was bordered by a sparse grass that accompanied it as far as the eye could see, in its disordered, breathless flow. I soon suggested to Maribé that we take a break beside the river. We still had to actually reach this alluring haven. I felt as if we were advancing toward a mirage that was fading as we approached.

Throughout our entire journey, I no longer spared a single thought for the region we'd left. I forced this void into my mind, saying that only at such a cost could I avoid regretting the decision I'd made. Christiane's voice sounded inside me, its echo permeating the whole forest. It was as if she were calling to us from far away. I imagined her alone, sitting in a corner, the way I'd left her, wondering to herself where we were right now. She must have been accompanying us in her mind, telling us which way to go, which path to take. We were walking straight ahead without looking back, rather like the way the whole village goes to the cemetery to pay a final tribute to someone who's died. On such an occasion the people of Batalébé don't look behind them. It's said that those who ignore this prohibition lose their sight and their reason. Were we perhaps burying our past lives from Batalébé, so that we oughtn't to look behind us till we reached Louboulou?

The Rest Stop

We finally arrived at the banks of a river so bright and clear we could see the least somersault, the least breath through the gills, of the creatures that lived in it. Big carp with gleaming scales were surrounded by a multicolored galaxy of small, skittery fish. The first thing we did was quench our thirst, then plunge our road-numbed feet in the water, whose coolness and purity refreshed us.

Since morning I'd been carrying a heavy bundle of clothes and other essentials on my back; I dropped it on the bank. Then

I gathered some twigs at the foot of a baobab to make a fire so we could heat up the food we'd brought.

Under a flame tree there was a rock that the limba and okoumé cutters must have used to sharpen their axes, for its surface was polished and whitish. We sat on it, eating slices of plantain with groundnut paste. I'd taken the precaution of wrapping these provisions in cassava leaves, the way our grandmothers used to before they left very early in the morning to walk to their fields many kilometers away.

Once we'd eaten our fill, we stretched out under another flame tree. The interwoven branches and lush foliage spared us from the overwhelming swelter of the afternoon. We stayed there for half an hour, our eyes barely open. In my head I could hear the minutes being marked off in a sort of ticktock that matched the beating of my heart.

Maribé now lay motionless. I needed to occupy myself with something, to keep from falling asleep. That above all. So I studied the bark and then the branches of the tree under which we were resting. I watched birds, each more brightly colored than the last, worn out by the heat, their bills hanging open, landing with heavy wings in the crown of the tree. Some of them, their eyes darting this way and that, pecked insistently at the leaves and searched for broad, deep cavities in the trunk, which they seemed to be already familiar with. Once they'd checked that no other creatures in the vicinity were following their movements, they slipped inside. Others peered at us, disturbed by our presence in those parts. Alarmed, they imposed the full range of their voices on us in a cacophony of song.

The Apparition

Now my gaze was directed elsewhere, toward a point above me. In the distance I could see a ball of light that appeared, vanished, then reappeared, like a throng of stars.

After a short while I could no longer make out anything at all. I had the feeling that the trees were swirling ferociously, the way they do in a hurricane; that they were swinging their branches in the air; that they were about to come crashing down upon us.

It was at this dizzying moment that a voice commanded me to get up. A figure appeared in front of me. I had difficulty recognizing the man, whose features seemed fluid and only half formed. When they came into focus, I saw that he was tall; his jaw was set, his gaze inflamed, his face red with anger. He was wearing a military uniform with black lace-up boots. He was coming forward with a slow, assured step. He gripped a pistol in his right hand.

My heart began to beat very fast.

I knew him. I wasn't mistaken. I would have taken an oath. Staked our freedom against a return to Batalébé. I wanted to speak, to say a few words. The man was there, in front of me, his weapon now aimed at my daughter. He stopped, stood stock still, almost lifeless. He took two more steps. Now I could get a good look at him and bow to the facts: it was him, no one else, the man who had enthralled me in the North. Kimbembé, the man I'd married.

His voice echoed in my head. How had he been able to trace our steps? Had he been lying in wait for us after he left the house on the eve of our departure? There were so many questions to which I had no answers. We no longer had any choice but to give ourselves up. All the same, I was sure we'd be offered a way out. For the moment we had to face my husband.

All at once his voice became sterner, resounding close to my ear like an ancient trumpet. Terrified, I leaped to my feet; I couldn't understand how my daughter and I had found ourselves here, by the banks of a river in a forest of the South. As if by magic, the figure of Kimbembé disappeared behind the flame trees. I realized that exhaustion had gotten the better of me. I was still shaking from the vision that had sprung from my own imagination.

Maribé was facing away from me. Her body arched backwards, she was asleep, lulled by the lapping sound of the river and the pleasant sensation of little droplets of water splashing on our faces.

She murmured some indistinct words; then finally she got up.

III

The Opportunity

The night before we left, I didn't sleep a wink. I was filled with anxiety as I awaited the moment. I got Maribé up when the first roosters of Batalébé were crowing.

She rubbed her eyes, still asleep and in the grip of a dream that she couldn't seem to shake off. She stood up, tottered, then turned like a puppet toward the kitchen, where she hurriedly plunged her head into a basin of water.

"It's going to be a long, long journey, but we'll make it to Louboulou," I said.

Kimbembé had not slept at home. He'd had to attend a meeting of the Negro Grandsons of Vercingetorix. Their gatherings, which he never missed these days, went on till the following day, and I knew he wouldn't come back before the evening, because he had to stay for hours on end to carry out an assessment of their operations that was held at the Palaver House, the regular meeting place of their movement, located on the market square. For that reason we had the time to gather our things together and leave. We would have to avoid the highway that splits the territory of the South in two and take all kinds of precautions so no one in Batalébé would see us leave. True, the highway hasn't been used by a single vehicle since the events in Mapapouville. I remember that in the days when my husband and I first came to this district, by day or by night we would count the big trucks, loaded with merchandise and with passengers crammed in like sardines, the bravest ones outside clinging to the tarpaulin, zooming by with their dodgy brakes. They'd kick up trails of red dust that would cover the vegetation along the way. Every so often an ill-fated sheep would dart from the bushes with its young and end up under the wheels of one of these vehicles, while its distraught offspring remained rooted to the spot at the side of the road. Then shirtless barefoot urchins, who were always on the lookout for such happenings, would run up laughing and throw themselves into the dust. They'd take the animal away, cut it up, then grill it and wolf it down in some clearing, far from the eyes of the adults.

Preparations

Our things, bundled together in an old wrap dress tied up with a piece of string, had been collected the previous evening and left by the door. They consisted of a jumble of food, clothes, Maribé's sandals, my high heels that I hadn't worn in ages but kept under the bed, candles, a box of matches, a few cooking pots, aluminum plates, soap, two drinking cups, two toothbrushes, an old tube of Émail Diamant toothpaste.

In a plastic bag I hid our birth certificates, my ID card, my high school diploma, and the photograph of Gaston and Christiane, along with the only letter sent by Léopold Mpassi-Mpassi, Christiane's brother, from France. I didn't forget the little Philips radio that today enables me to follow events, even if the information comes from the victors. I took the old notebooks in which I'd already begun to recount the Mapapouville events. I dusted them off after glancing through the opening pages of each one. I noticed, not without an inner satisfaction, that each period of the events was clearly recorded in some place or other. I almost burned them when I was making the final arrangements, thinking they would only add more weight to the burden I was going to have to lug all day, all the way to Louboulou. But that would have felt like a setback. I would have lost the traces of my own existence. Why destroy these documents after I'd kept them safe all this time under Kimbembé's big trunk of books, in a corner of the bedroom, a poorly lit spot whose clutter discouraged anyone from venturing into it?

The metal trunk was padlocked, dusty, and in time it had grown prey to rust. Kimbembé claimed half-jokingly that it was older than Maribé, maybe even older than me. He'd inherited it when his grandfather died. In it he kept his French, geography, and history course materials, and textbooks on these subjects. Some of the materials dated from his first steps in the profession, from the time he'd been posted to Oweto, my home village in the North. There were also French novels that long ago he'd urged me to read. Quite a few of them had no cover, including *The Red and the Black*, *The Thief's Journal*, *The Plague*, *Book of My Mother*, *The Hunchback of Notre-Dame*, and *Eugénie Grandet*. Without a cover it was hard for me to know the author's name. So Kimbembé explained to me that such and such a book was by Stendhal, another by Genet, others still by Camus, Cohen, Hugo, or Balzac. He maintained that if you hear even a single word by an author, you ought to be able to guess who it's by if you've read at least one of that writer's books. He helped me to understand that a person can love books with a love as deep as that felt for another human being. "Reading, like any act of love," he would say, "requires tenderness, sensitivity, and originality. You need to woo a book the same way you woo a woman, up to the point where you win it over and you can live with it, for better or for worse." He said too that for a man reading a beautiful book and a man making love to a woman he loves, the heart beats in the same way: his breath comes in gasps, his blood flows uneasily right up until the final rapture, when, after he climaxes, his muscles relax. He had a saying on this topic: "Marriage with books is the only form of union that does not suffer from the crime of adultery." In addition he shared his love of books, spread it about by lending them to his students and his colleagues in the North.

Panic

I finished gathering our things late in the night. I wanted to take only what was essential. Everything seemed important, to the point that I went back and forth for several minutes before making up my mind. Plus, I needed to ensure that I wouldn't be loaded down.

All the same, panic began to get the better of me.

A voice that came from my conscience tried to hold me back in the house. Yet the wish to leave it, to flee this environment, asserted itself. It was a decision weighty in consequences for my daughter and me, but I could no longer back down. I had to be decisive, tell myself that it was today or never.

IV

The Forbidden Visit

Christiane alone knew that our departure was imminent. We'd spoken about it. Actually, on that day the two of us talked more than at any time since we'd known each other. Or rather, I contented myself with listening to her, since I didn't believe we'd have another chance to see one another.

* * *

I didn't notice the time passing, the night falling. Maribé must have been worried by my long absence—I'd promised her I wouldn't stay more than two hours at Christiane's. At worst, she knew how much she'd be able to get done if I stayed longer: she could sweep the yard, because I preferred doing it in the evening so as not to have to get up early in the morning; close the chicken coop behind the house because of hungry big cats on the prowl in the neighborhood; go buy a liter of kerosene from old Madame Niangui for our two hurricane lamps; and also close the windows and the door and wait for me to come back.

I knew full well that Kimbembé might come home early and find her there alone. But the chances of that happening were slim. I was sure of it, the more so because the evening before my visit to Christiane I'd seen my husband on the other side of the bedroom, very late at night, diligently sorting documents that were to be handed out during the scheduled meeting at the Palaver House. So he couldn't possibly come back before midnight. That kind of meeting would be followed by the Negro Grandsons of Vercingetorix visiting different strategic points in the region or going to their headquarters, situated somewhere in the depths of the forest, in a secret location guarded by trusted men who were under orders not to think, not to leave their post even for a second, to open fire even on leaves falling from the trees. On the main square we'd see men going by dressed in military-style uniforms. They would search houses, threatening the inhabitants and confiscating their shotguns: Vercingetorix was in the vicinity and was going to speak to his Negro Grandsons. Shots would be fired in the air. The local people would be overcome by dread. We said among ourselves that perhaps this was the moment the powers of Mapapouville had chosen to put an end to things. Then the guns would fall silent. A Peugeot 504 with tinted windows would drive along the highway, escorted by a stream of Land Rovers. The soldiers wore sunglasses, their red berets pulled down over their eyebrows. They would indulge in a parade. Vercingetorix would get out of the Peugeot, encircled by twenty or so bodyguards who would go stand outside and wait for the end of the meeting, which sometimes went on till the next day.

The memory of the last time I saw Christiane still plucks at my heart. I don't dare imagine what will become of her in the months to come.

Right now I'm thinking of her. I sense her near me. She's whispering the words that I'm writing down here. I can see again the courage and the silence that characterized her. To me, Christiane is an exceptional woman, the kind of woman you only meet once in your life.

I wish she had said yes to the suggestion I made at that time, which she rejected forcefully: to come with us to Louboulou.

At the time, I could only see the upside in it for her. I hadn't counted on the attachment she had for the land of Batalébé. She felt it deep down inside herself as a way of being, something that brought harmony to her soul. To leave her birthplace would have meant erasing her self. Yet those were not her only arguments. I believe it was important to her to show Vercingetorix's men that even though they had taken every reason to live away from her, she wouldn't budge from her home. She would remain there, shut away, walled up, sitting or lying on the ground, as an appeal to their conscience. But did they *have* a conscience, the Negro Grandsons of Vercingetorix?

The Same Story

The day of farewell, an unforgettable day.

I was by her. I had difficulty fixing her in my mind's eye, perhaps because I ceased to recognize this woman who was no longer entirely the same person and who from day to day, in solitude and contemplation, had to endure the burden of her fate like a kind of sword lodged in her back for many months.

What had happened to Christiane belonged to the realm of the unspeakable, the unbearable. Yet she spoke to me of it bravely and selflessly. True, during this farewell she repeated facts that I already knew, but this time it was in a particular voice and with a particular feeling, as if she were conveying her last wishes to me. On that day I did not for a moment allow myself to feel tired or irked at hearing the same story. Quite the opposite, I wanted to fill myself with it, to take it in, aware that I might never have another opportunity to hear her tell it to me again.

She raised her voice, getting carried away and growing defiant. Her speech came faster, and she let out all the hatred, all the resentment she harbored from her encounter with the Negro Grandsons of Vercingetorix.

An Out-of-the-Way House

We were sitting side by side.

At this point she was little more than a bundle of old clothes. As if she were punishing herself, convinced she was the cause of the treatment being meted out to Gaston Okemba, her husband, somewhere there in the bush.

She lived alone, like a childless widow, in that dilapidated, isolated house, which she had inherited from her mother. You had to go through a small woods and pass the Mampembé Cemetery. A building of baked clay stood there, topped by a metal roof. From a distance it looked like an abandoned storehouse. The lot was marked off by some rusty barbwire and a line of mango trees. From time to time, pigs spattered with kaolin would grunt back and forth to each other in the woods, walk upstream along the Léfini, then come and couple in the yard. The windows were always open, and also the door, which was held in place on the outside by a piece of red brick. The door could be closed from inside with a whittled piece of wood kept in place by a length of creeper tucked into a crack in the front wall. Termites built their rounded nests right on the rafters. Grass grew in front, and the yard was riddled with potholes.

So as not to be recognized on the day of that final visit, I wore a black scarf over my head. Kimbembé had forbidden me to go see Christiane anymore. Before I entered the lot, I looked back. No one had followed me. Few locals strayed as far as this house, except for the fishermen who would set their hoop nets in the Léfini late at night. From her place Christiane would hear them passing in a group. A dozen or so men who would rummage in the innards of this watercourse, supposedly a haven for the *Mami Wata*, half-women, half-fish, who according to local belief emerge from the water in the middle of the night and spend hours combing their long silver hair on the riverbank. These apparitions come out during a full moon. If there's ever more of a crowd than usual by the river in the morning, it's because the villagers dream of finding a comb left behind by a *Mami Wata*. Such an object is said to cure a multitude of ills. It also offers protection against evil spirits, attracts prosperity, and guarantees a long life.

A Diminished Woman

I rounded the lot as if I were heading for the Léfini. I moved aside some strips of barbwire and found myself in front of the half-broken door. I gave a first knock.

There was no response.

I stood there for a few minutes, wondering whether I'd have to turn around and go back home. I had to see Christiane. I couldn't leave Batalébé without seeing and hearing her. I knew she'd talk, that she'd take the time for that.

I knocked again.

At last I heard slow, irregular footsteps, like those of someone who has trouble getting around. A faint cough, then a barely audible voice. She peered through one of the chinks in the door. Her shadow shifting, her head shaved, her wrap dress and camisole stained with red earth—Christiane was there.

Her forehead was drawn and her gaze absent; her eyes spun till they came to rest on me with a cadaverous stillness.

She closed the door behind me after fighting like a she-devil with the little piece of wood that served as a key, and invited me to sit down on a mat. A bowl of groundnuts lay on the floor.

"You're here? What's wrong? Who saw you on the way?" she said.

"Everyone's in the center of Batalébé," I replied. "There's a meeting at the Palaver House, so I—"

"Be careful all the same!" she broke in. "They're everywhere since Vercingetorix came back to Batalébé."

She shook the groundnuts in the bowl as if she were counting them, tossing out the nuts that were damaged. From time to time she pushed her thumb into her nose, digging for the mucus that obstructed her breathing.

"Recently," she went on, "they've been talking about your family. I see everything from here, even though I don't leave the house anymore. They think your husband is setting a bad example. You're a problem for them, and you should be aware of it . . ."

I didn't react, but I paid close attention to what she was saying. She broke up a few nuts and started trying to wipe the red dust off her top. She gave the impression of no longer caring about life in the slightest.

"Christiane, I'm more afraid for you, and—"

"I'm no longer afraid of anything after what I went through," she interrupted. "I ask myself whether I even deserve the air I breathe. I've had enough of it all! They took Gaston away because he's from the North! And since I'm their 'sister' from the South, they've always seen it as a double treachery—I married that man and then had the temerity to bring him to our region. No one had the guts to intervene. They're all cowards."

"I'm in almost the same situation!" I retorted.

"Let's agree it's a little different. Kimbembé can breathe easy because he became a militant. Plus, the Negro Grandsons need guys like him who have studied. That's why they leave him the hell alone. I'm sure he's already being pressured. A militant has to show an example to others. Whereas he has a wife from the North! What a betrayal!"

She waited to see how I'd react. I lowered my eyes.

"I know you have a reason for coming here, Hortense. Tell me everything. You and I have never hidden anything from each other. I can see you're not your usual self!"

"The thing is . . ."

"You don't need to justify yourself. You've come to say good-bye to me. You've decided to run away from this land of fanatics. I even think you've waited too long. But I'm glad to see you've made up your mind. Now is the time when you have to assume your responsibilities."

"Actually, Kimbembé is going away next week, but I'm scared that—"

"What do you mean, scared! You should be looking for a means to escape. And any means is good. You're a threat; Kimbembé isn't brave enough to say it to your face—he's as much of a coward as the rest of them. Think of Maribé, who's completely blameless in all this, and remember that Gaston too was blameless."

"Where am I supposed to go? I don't know anywhere else in the South aside from Batalébé, and my home village is six hundred miles away!"

After a fit of coughing, Christiane went on in a husky voice: "I've talked to you a few times about Pointe-Rouge, the financial capital . . . Well, that's the only solution for you and your daughter. You need to go through Pointe-Rouge, there's nothing else for it . . ."

"But Pointe-Rouge is the opposite direction from my region!"

"The roads leading directly to the North are controlled by the Negro Grandsons. Your escape will have to be made in stages . . ."

"Meaning?" I replied sharply.

In my head I'd already come up with all kinds of routes. The idea of going directly to Pointe-Rouge had crossed my mind. It's a big city where there would soon be opportunities to return to my native region. I'd heard about the old Antonov planes that plied the skies above Vietongo and had saved the lives of many from the North. But I'd also heard tell of the traps that the Negro Grandsons' accomplices cooked up for northerners. They pretended to be loyal transporters, working for the Russians who secured the rare shuttle flights between the two extremities of the country. These people spoke fluent Russian, and so the travelers felt safe and climbed on board for a destination that only became apparent when the plane landed in the middle of the forest. Furthermore, taking the highway directly to Pointe-Rouge would have exposed us to another danger. When Vercingetorix's men decide to go hunting fugitives, they begin by flying over the main highway in helicopters, finding those fleeing stretched out in single file along the side of the road.

"No!" Christiane exclaimed, interrupting my thoughts. "Above all you shouldn't take the highway; that's a mistake you mustn't make. To the southwest of Batalébé there's a village called Louboulou. Not many people know it. It's a backwater, the most secluded place in the South. No one goes there, and the inhabitants take themselves for ghosts. It's in the middle of nowhere, an elephant cemetery, a forgotten corner of the map. But it's an ideal place to hide out and then later head for Pointe-Rouge. The village is a day's walk from here—Gaston and I passed through there one time. The only reference point I can give you is that Crayfish Creek runs through it. If you find the creek, you'll be within a stone's throw of Louboulou. And if I remember correctly, there's a cemetery not far from the creek."

The Photograph

Forgetting for a moment that Christiane was talking to me, I thought about certain things my husband had said, about his favorite insult, which he repeated like a leitmotif and which now echoed in my head: "Those northern dogs are back, we can't have that."

Coming back to reality, I chased my wandering thoughts away with the back of my hand. To show my friend I'd been listening to her, I put in: "Why don't you leave Batalébé with us?"

Her gaze shifted to the window, toward the Mampembé Cemetery. She passed a hand over her bare skull and studied me before replying in a serious and firm tone that told me she'd been expecting my question.

"I was born here, they know it. I have nothing more to lose. The graves of my parents are in this earth. To leave here would be to betray the man who they've unjustly taken prisoner and who I still love. It would be to deny my origins. What has Gaston been accused of? Nothing!"

I turned in the direction of her bedroom. I saw the rickety little table that was the only piece of furniture left in the house after the Negro Grandsons had come. The faint light filtering through gaps in the window frame fell on a framed black-and-white photograph that stood on the table. Christiane had only taken the picture out a few days ago—I hadn't seen it on my previous visits. I recognized the couple in the picture: Christiane had her Angela Davis Afro, and Gaston, with his neatly trimmed mustache, had just burst out laughing, which made the whole picture more cheerful despite the stiff expression of his wife.

I lingered over the image of Gaston.

"What's the latest about him?" I asked, pointing to the photograph.

After a long pause she answered in a resigned voice.

"Right now I'm convinced that the worst has happened. The day before yesterday, 'those people' came all the way here to see me, and they offered me a sum of money. I refused such a tainted gift. I wanted to see him, if only for fifteen minutes. They told me that was impossible. Each time they come, it's someone different. When they left they jumped into a jeep that was waiting there in front of the lot."

She abruptly fell silent and shook her head a few times, trying to rid herself of the images of her existence that were passing before her. She rose swiftly and crossed to the little table. She picked up the photograph, gazed lovingly at it, then cleaned the corners of the frame with her spit and polished the glass on the side of the picture showing her husband.

"The more I clean his face, the more he smiles—see!"

I nodded without getting up. She came back to my side, tears in her eyes. Pushing aside the bowl of nuts, she stretched out her legs and ground her teeth. She leaned back against the wall, pressing the photograph against her chest with all her might. She closed her eyes, utterly lost in thought.

She really needed to be left alone with this backward gaze that was carrying her far, far away among her memories, to each one of our meetings. She was seeing herself years before. And also her man Gaston, her late mother and father, her unappreciative brother Léopold Mpassi-Mpassi, her in-laws, her life in Pointe-Rouge.

None of it was foreign to me anymore. I'd grown to know the streets of Pointe-Rouge, the life in its neighborhoods. I felt close to this city that she glorified. I became a little girl again whenever she told me about her life in the financial capital.

V

A Surge of Memories

That day of farewell was no longer like the other days, when we could give free rein to our outbursts of laughter. In front of me was a mere shadow of a woman. Yet her face was lit by a kind of glow, and she didn't need to speak—we communicated otherwise. It was for that reason I watched her, imagining to myself the turmoil of her thoughts. This same story she was telling me: she had no idea that one day I'd write it down in my notebook.

Gaston's Arrest

In her confusion of thoughts, Christiane for sure began by remembering the arrest of Gaston Okemba, and then the following day, when the Negro Grandsons had returned late at night to administer their "correction," as the local expression went. In Batalébé everyone was familiar with this episode in her life. It all went back to the first punitive acts by the Negro Grandsons of Vercingetorix: Christiane and Gaston were among the first to suffer the consequences of events that were taking place in Mapapouville, our political capital.

At the time it happened, she had refrained from telling me. It wasn't out of embarrassment. She had worried about making me distrustful, about putting me in a state of permanent suspicion. Later she'd realized that, like the other inhabitants,

I must have heard rumors—all the rumors going around the district. So at that point she'd wanted to establish the truth, tell me her own version of events, even if it meant making me anxious. I didn't see her till a week after the "visit" by the Negro Grandsons of Vercingetorix. She was curled up in her bedroom, no longer opening the door to anyone. In a flat voice she told me that the Negro Grandsons had turned up outside their house in the middle of the night. A light rain was pattering on the metal roof, and the wind blew in intermittent but strong gusts over Batalébé. One jeep pulled up by the front yard, another a little farther off, both with their lights out. Men carrying flashlights and armed with pistols and shotguns kicked in the front door. At first Christiane and Gaston were so shocked they thought it was a nightmare. The men who had broken into their home all wore balaclavas, and at no point did any one of them utter a single word. They communicated through gestures, training their guns on the couple. Christiane and Gaston knew that a single cry from either of them would have been enough to prompt a gunshot. So above all they had to stay calm. They had to let their "visitors" do what they were going to do, and try to understand why. It wasn't easy. Aggression showed in every movement these men made. Underneath their masks, Christiane could tell they were inflamed with hatred and rage.

There were more than half a dozen Negro Grandsons of Vercingetorix inside the house. One of them, seemingly their commanding officer, nodded to the couple to move apart. Gaston begged Christiane to do what she was told; it was all a big mistake that he would clear up with them. The officer, incensed, pressed the barrel of his gun against Gaston's forehead. There hadn't been any mistake, and he would have to go with them, or they'd carry him out feet first. Christiane was beside herself.

"Who do you think you are? This is our home. Get out!"

"Right, this is your home," the officer said sarcastically, throwing his mask to the ground in a nervous impulse.

His circumflex-shaped mustache twitched in anger. The slap he gave Christiane sent her staggering to the other side of the bamboo bed. As she crumpled to the ground, she knocked over a little stand with three shelves on which she kept her toiletries and a few knickknacks. The clatter of the breaking objects drew the attention of another masked man, more single-minded than the first, who burst into the bedroom. He pushed his associates aside. He wanted to get the job done quickly. Without a word he raised his submachine gun high in the air and smashed the butt down on Gaston's head. Gaston instantly slumped to the floor, unconscious.

During this time, other men who were posted by the door, aided outside by moving shapes whose presence could barely be made out, had formed a line and were removing the furniture from the house and carrying it toward the two vehicles. In no time at all the Formica-topped table, the carved chairs, the meat safe, the kitchen dresser, the radio, the black-and-white TV set, the tape player, the big hanging mirror by the window—all had disappeared. The living room was emptied out. The rats and the cockroaches, whose presence had been legitimized by these objects, made a rush for the kitchen.

Christiane was shouting herself hoarse, calling in vain for help. The rain was now pouring down. Gaston, his head covered in blood, was dragged across the floor as far as the living room, limp and still out cold. Two men tried to pick him up. The stronger of the two told the other man to step aside and let him handle it. He grabbed the northerner by the belt and, with a sudden jerk, hoisted him in the air. Gaston landed on the shoulders of the masked giant, who lugged him outside. In desperation Christiane sprang out of the bedroom like a wounded big cat and pushed one of the Negro Grandsons against the wall.

She tore his face with her nails. She received another slap from the officer; the house seemed to spin, and the men were now no more than blurry images. The officer accused her of being a traitor and promised that other Negro Grandsons would deal with her in the coming hours, that she would regret bringing her "northern scum" to the district of Batalébé.

The two vehicles roared off, their lights still out, their wheels splashing through the mud. Christiane got to her feet and for a long time walked around outside in hopes of finding help. She would have had to run for half an hour at least. The jeeps were already rumbling through the Mampembé Cemetery, heading for the highway that led out of the district. Lightning struck the top of the highest tree in the vicinity; then there was a crash of thunder. Helpless, Christiane sprawled in the mud and yielded to the hypocritical rain as it beat down on her.

The Correction

Five Negro Grandsons had come back to "correct" her. Christiane had not moved from her house. She'd left the disorder from the previous night as it was. She recognized the officer by his short stature and his drooping mustache. How could she have slept the night they took Gaston away? She couldn't get the images of the men beating him out of her mind. She remembered that after the Negro Grandsons had left with her husband she had felt vanquished; she'd run out into the rain and sprawled on the ground. She'd lacked the strength to get back up, or even to call for help. Crawling back to the house, she'd bumped up against the boards of the broken door that she was no longer able to close. She'd also noticed boot prints, and Gaston's blood on the front of the house. The shadows of "those men" seemed to be everywhere. But she wanted to confront them, so she sat down on the living room floor. She put her legs together, rested her chin on her knees, and closed her eyes till morning. In her weakened condition, she'd seen the sun rise in a state of confusion then set slowly, like a boa that had been deceived by the large size of its prey and was now reduced to a few convulsive movements.

On the morning after the abduction of her husband, she hadn't heard a single sound around her. The day had come and gone as if nothing had happened. The few birds to be seen—crows—flew low over the roof of the house or perched in the tops of the mango trees in the neighborhood. For Christiane these were clear omens: these birds, in the traditions of the south of Vietongo, symbolize mourning, misfortune. With their rasping voices they broadcast bad news. On that day no one crossed the river. In this way the entire district had consigned Christiane to complete isolation. Where could she have gone to complain without making those she spoke to burst out laughing? Since the events in Mapapouville, we no longer had any representative of public authority left in the district, or for that matter anywhere else in the South.

* * *

The Negro Grandsons had come back the following evening to administer a "correction." The threats of the previous day had not intimidated her in any way. Quite the opposite, she'd begged to be taken to where they were holding her husband.

The Negro Grandsons found Christiane there, sitting in the living room, in the same position as when they'd left the day before. She had the feeling that her blood had stopped circulating, that her heart had slowed. She felt sharp pains in her joints, and her feet were numb.

After Christiane's "correction" by the Negro Grandsons, I began to ask myself questions about the future of my marriage with Kimbembé. I imagined myself in my friend's place, faced with these men who had decided to pursue their objectives to the very end. Their actions were of such barbarity that even in this notebook I've had to erase several passages. Christiane would never once have considered letting someone abuse her body in such a way. On that night she shook with hatred, rage, and frustration. Her body belonged to a pack of stinking hyenas. She saw the mustache of the commanding officer coming close to her face to kiss her greedily. His breath was rancid; he must have been chewing moldy tobacco, garlic, leeks, cola nuts. His coated tongue passed over her lips, and Christiane felt as if an icy centipede were probing her mouth. She wanted to bite this flesh that lay motionless against her palate, but her strength had long ago abandoned her. The man defiled her, repeating the word *traitor* right up till the moment he let out an animalistic groan of climax, then got up, unburdened now and cheerful, his khaki pants around his ankles. He gave the order to another man, then another again, to repeat the same task.

Falling Apart

Since that wretched day—that day of degradation—Christiane completely ceased to feel herself a woman. She resolved to abandon anything that recalled her physical beauty or gave men the idea of chasing around after her. From that moment on, the men of the district disgusted her. She was convinced that the face of each of them could be that of the officer, whose features she had not been fully able to make out, and who had held on to her, panting like a rutting stag. Any short-statured man she saw revolted her. Her whole body would start trembling. At the sight of such a stranger, a man in the street, she felt the need to vomit, though she would get a grip on herself in time. She was no longer any more than filth—she who had once been tall and graceful, with her brown skin and the small of her back that gave rise to the boldest conversations in Batalébé. Most, if not all, of the men in the district had at least once fantasized about having her in their bed. Christiane was an upright and faithful woman. Faithful to her husband, faithful to their love. It was appalling to see how a human being could fall apart in the space of a few months, then totally collapse. She took it out on herself, on the body that had betrayed her by receiving the sticky sap of the little man with the mustache, the commanding officer, then that of the other Negro Grandsons of Vercingetorix. She had to erase the stigma of these blemishes on her skin. To no longer be the same debased woman—that was her intent. She had thought about washing herself for an entire day in the Léfini. That would not have sufficed. What she wanted was a visible transformation. So she shaved her head, cutting off her beautiful silky black hair. Her eyebrows too. She kept pressing her nose with her thumb to make it flatter. She let the dirt harden under her fingernails, which she stopped trimming. She barely ate anything and grew thinner by the day, as if she were already in mourning for her husband, because in Batalébé a widow has to withdraw herself from the community. According to the customs of the South, after her husband dies a wife is expected to stop paying any attention to her grooming. This means no longer brushing her teeth, looking at herself in the mirror, washing with soap, combing her hair, wearing sandals or earrings. With her odor she should repel anyone who draws near, especially men.

And so Christiane went barefoot, eyes lowered and turning away; she wore tattered black or crimson clothes that trailed in the red dust of her yard. Some widows still lead such an existence in the district. Their beauty withers in less than a week, like a fruit rotting prematurely. In fact, Christiane must have thought of her own mother, who lived like that following the death of her spouse.

After Gaston's abduction, Christiane had resolved to live an austere life. In her mind, Gaston was no longer of this world. Vercingetorix's men said that she'd gone mad and that no one had arrested her northerner husband. He'd fled of his own accord, they claimed, in the night, so as to join the camp of the victors in Mapapouville. The Negro Grandsons lectured the local inhabitants: harboring a northerner would rebound on you in the end; you ran the risk of being betrayed one day. Especially because Gaston had worked at the Moukoukoulou Dam, an important strategic point in the region.

The Infertile Woman

Neither the fetid smell in her house nor the fact that she looked like a madwoman would have put me off going to see her. She remained my friend, my best friend, if not the only one I had in the district. We'd known each other since my arrival in Batalébé. Not because her husband was from the same region as me, but because I felt I could trust her. It was even more than friendship, in that land where I was somewhat isolated. We would braid each other's hair once a month—back then Kimbembé had no objection to my spending time with her. Sometimes we would buy identical wrap dresses, earrings, or necklaces and head over to the big market in Batalébé, where we'd met for the first time. Deep inside me I cherish the image from those days of Christiane's hand stroking my braids and touching Maribé's cheek.

I admit, and still regret, that I was reluctant to take Maribé with me when I went to her house. Yet I had a reason that might have served as justification. The times I went to see her with my daughter, Christiane kept staring at her. I imagined what was going through her mind: she was sorrowful at not having been able to bring a child into the world. Not having experienced the happiness of being a mother. Her infertility grieved her. Her mother had made her drink the bitterest concoctions, whose virtues had been known since the beginning of the world, but to no avail. Christiane had tried everything. She and Gaston had consulted the most renowned healers in Batalébé and even throughout the South. Nothing could be done. The spirits had turned her ovaries upside down and knotted them seventy-seven times, concluded these men who possessed the power to stop the rain, to make it fall in the middle of the dry season, or to question a dead person in his coffin until he gave his mourners the address of the man or woman who had been the cause of his death.

Patient Gaston consoled her in her moments of bitterness. The failure did not originate with him—that much had been established by the most trustworthy doctors of the Adolphe-Cissé Hospital in Pointe-Rouge. For all that, he wasn't tempted to go elsewhere. Quite the opposite, he grew closer to Christiane, but that didn't help to ease his wife's distress. She believed that a love so intense ought to be rewarded with the arrival of a little angel. She held it against herself when she saw a woman carrying a baby on her back, or a pregnant woman. She struck her belly, insulted it. Each month she cried at the first drops of her period. She railed against the natural cycle that reminded her she would never know the three dry trimesters during which a little being is made in the intimacy of the umbilical cord and the amniotic fluid. For her, the worst part was that when Gaston seemed quiet and distant, she imagined it was because of her childlessness. She didn't dare ask him about it. She knew Gaston didn't like to make a big deal of it. She would leave the house and walk alone by the Léfini, tears in her eyes.

VI

A Sunday to Remember

Christiane liked telling me the story of her romance with Gaston. There was a kind of exultation that filled her when she revisited those times. She had a special way of insisting on the details, of acting out the events, riveting my attention. She told me everything without reserve, spiritedly, from the second time we met at her place to braid our hair as we had the previous month.

That had been several years ago. During our farewell she must have been thinking about that Sunday afternoon. We'd only just gotten to know each other, yet it didn't bother her at all to tell me all about Gaston and her. While I hadn't told her a thing about married life with Kimbembé!

A Sunday to remember. Christiane was radiant. She talked and talked. We were sitting in raffia chairs behind their house, in the shade of the mango trees that mark the edge of their yard. It was in September. Gaston was at work at the Moukoukoulou Dam. As she braided my hair with adept, gentle movements, she spoke to me about Pointe-Rouge, giving my head a little shake from time to time to make sure I was listening. It's true that I sometimes happened to doze off while her long, slender fingers moved softly in my hair, or as she dexterously parted it into rows using a porcupine quill.

The Lovers of Pointe-Rouge

It was in Pointe-Rouge that they had met. Gaston was working at the seaport, one of the biggest in the central part of the continent. Christiane was a clerk at the Main Post Office, opposite the train station. Nothing indicated a long-term relationship. They crossed paths on their way to their respective places of work downtown. They took the same bus each morning; Gaston would get on a few stops after Christiane. "When you see someone every day, at the same time, in the same place, they become familiar," she asserted. "And the day you don't see them at all, you ask yourself questions. Did he go to work earlier than usual? Is he off today? Is he sick?"

When they saw each other again, after this break that had in fact only lasted a day or two, each of them had at a distance hidden their delight at seeing the other. Christiane no longer remembered the exact moment when they'd started to say good morning to one another. First with a nod of the head, she recollected vaguely. Then with a handshake, and finally with a brief exchange of words. On several occasions Gaston had gallantly offered her his seat on the bus, an uncommon gesture in the *fula-fulas* and even the *cent-cents* of Pointe-Rouge, in which men have no scruples about jostling women, shouldering ahead of them as they get on so as to grab the most comfortable places. Christiane had been touched. To begin with she refused his offer; then she relented when Gaston insisted. In fact this courtesy troubled her; she felt she didn't deserve it from someone she didn't know well and only met by chance on her way to work. Were there ulterior motives in the attentions of this distinguished-looking young man? She didn't dare believe it. It all seemed so real and natural that no actor could have performed so well. Some days she preferred to travel standing up, by the side of the young man, as far as downtown. She gave up her seat to another woman or an elderly person, who thanked her profusely.

Their talk remained polite, with a certain reserve. They were aware of never going to the heart of things, of avoiding a reality that was staring them in the face. It was like a watercourse that had to be crossed, with each of them on a different side, counting on the other to make the leap.

According to Christiane, Gaston was more bashful than she was. It was a bashfulness that he hid masterfully beneath an animation that allowed him to find topics to enliven any conversation. At such moments he would launch into long explanations in a scholarly tone of voice, making gestures of studied precision. When he mentioned books he'd read, it was hard to see it as pretentious. Everything seemed appropriate. Sometimes he'd bring up an example from La Fontaine's *Fables*, several of which he knew by heart. The same went for the songs of Georges Brassens, which he would hum in a labored voice. Christiane had been spellbound the day the young man had recited one of the best-known of La Fontaine's fables, "The Oak and the Reed." "He read a lot, and dreamed of writing books," Christiane said. He had produced piles of short stories, poems, and plays, but he came to the conviction that, although he had the will, the talent was missing, and that a person didn't become a writer just by reading books.

"If you lack talent, you need modesty enough to read the work of others," he would declare with a bitter expression.

The moment he fell silent, Christiane would be struck by his inward-looking, introverted nature, which made her think that this man from the North was a fragile being, extremely cautious in his relations with the opposite sex. But he gave the impression of being rather considerate, attentive, and kind, in a way that could be sensed at once in his manner of smiling, of saying hello: he would put his hand on his chest, over his heart, and bow almost to the ground. During a conversation he would nod his head, reassuring his interlocutor, helping in the choice of words or images. When he said good-bye he would place his hand on his heart again and turn back several times with a string of polite words.

The Singer Sewing Machine

Christiane and Gaston could have spent months sizing each other up like that. Things sped up thanks to a Singer sewing machine. This object came to symbolize their growing relationship. I can't resist telling the story of the Singer here, the more so because Christiane spoke about it at length the day we said farewell.

Christiane didn't see how things could have come about without the sewing machine. Gaston was afraid in advance of being awkward, and he held back, whereas Christiane for her part could not make the first move, something unthinkable for a woman, she told herself. Besides, what would Gaston have thought of her if she'd gone on the attack? She was hoping that Gaston would be more open, more willing. He, on the other hand, was scared of displeasing this young woman, who may have seen their relationship simply as friendship. Each time he decided that he'd push forward, that he'd take the plunge at the next opportunity, the words stuck in his throat in Christiane's presence. And he said nothing, gazing at her as if begging her to understand his message by telepathy. Christiane would lower her eyes; the *fula-fula* or the *cent-cent* would stop downtown. They'd get off, say their good-byes with a handshake. She would cross Tchicaya U Tam'si Boulevard, aware that Gaston was watching her. She didn't turn around. And the young man would come to the conclusion that they were not thinking the same thing.

The Customs Officers of Pointe-Rouge

Christiane had gone to the seaport of Pointe-Rouge to take delivery of a Singer sewing machine that she'd ordered from abroad. It had taken more than three months by cargo ship. She'd given up hope, till one day she received notification that it had arrived. That didn't mean the battle was over: she would have to grease the palms of several customs officers to pick up her package the same day. In Pointe-Rouge everyone abides by this tradition. That is how the officers make ends meet, and many of them boast they earn more money like that than from their regular monthly salary. So for them, someone coming to pick up a package was a stroke of luck. They would surround the person, trail around after them. The addressee would have to traipse from one office to the next, not forgetting the security officers, who, if they were weren't happy, could make the merchandise vanish in the space of a few seconds. All they needed was to whistle to their colleagues and the job was done.

On that day Christiane had understood that knowing people in the administration makes things easier. It saves you from the overexcited women counter clerks and the security officers sniffing around. You're brought through a side door, unseen by those standing in line, who have been waiting for hours and who have need of even more patience when at midday they hear, from a clerk more interested in what he's going to have for lunch, that their package is not available and that they should come back early the next morning.

"What do you mean, the package is unavailable?"

"Like I said."

"But I can see it right there on the shelf behind you!"

"There's no need to be difficult. It's unavailable. You need to leave, or it'll be three months before you get it!"

Christiane had not had to face such a disappointment. Gaston had come up when he saw her crossing the courtyard that led to the Central Customs Office, that famous part of the seaport where transactions were only ever accomplished by wetting the beard of the clerks and where there was always an inordinate concentration of customs officers per square yard. In a few minutes she'd picked up her Singer. She hadn't paid a penny. Gaston had turned down the thousand-franc banknote she'd offered for him to go wet his beard in a downtown bar. They talked instead about eating together one weekday during their midday break.

The meal took place a few days later, in a little *nganda* in the Trois-Cents neighborhood, opposite the Rex Cinema.

A Failed Writer

The day of our farewell, Christiane brought up that memorable Sunday when, in between two braids that she was knotting in my hair, she'd told me how everything had subsequently progressed very quickly between her and Gaston. When she was with him she felt a power, a warmth running through her body. She imagined having already known him in a previous life. He was tall, with fine features and a mustache he trimmed with scissors almost hair by hair. He articulated clearly, careful to be understood, in a generous, melodious accent associated with the northerners of Vietongo. She valued his sophistication, his knowledge. For her, Gaston was a failed writer because of his perfectionism and his devotion to the great French authors. How could he fully pursue his passion when after every line he wrote, he would stop and declare that Balzac, Proust, and Montherlant had already written everything, in beautiful, elegant, incomparable language that was fixed for all eternity? Sitting in his office, gazing into space, he spent more time ripping his work up than actually writing. He would rise to his feet, stretch, and gaze through the window at the sea. He must have been asking himself what he was doing in that room filled with documents, which he would gladly have lined with books.

Gaston's Family

Since the beginning of their relationship, Gaston had stressed to Christiane that he was from the North, mindful of the reactions he had met with from other young women in Pointe-Rouge, the emblematic city of the South. Christiane had responded by saying that she didn't see how this information was helpful. The young man's journey fascinated her, for he and his parents had come from far away. It was at the time when Pointe-Rouge was the Peru of Vietongo. People say that in those days everything seemed simple. No obstacles stood between people. Gaston had been living in Pointe-Rouge for many years, having arrived from the North at a young age with his parents after Vietongo became independent. He had gone to school there, attending Savorgnan-de-Brazza Middle School and Monseigneur-Carrie High School, from which he received his baccalaureate in literature. But then he'd entered the Customs School—was this a sign of destiny?—right opposite the Main Post Office, where Christiane would come to work a few years later, and after that he got a job with Customs Regional Management, in the Department of Inspection and Control at the Port of Pointe-Rouge.

From that point on, thanks to his job, Gaston gradually became independent from his family. He rented two rooms in a neighborhood on the edge of the city. That did not relieve him of the obligation of looking after his mother, father, and two younger brothers. He would go see them on Sunday afternoons. He never regarded those visits as a duty. He was close to his family—his mother, whose eyesight was failing as she grew older, and his father, who worked at the Pointe-Rouge morgue.

Basile Okemba was a famous figure in the city of Pointe-Rouge. No one challenged him or disrespected him. He would respond to his detractors by saying: "For the moment you can strut about insulting me. I'll be waiting for you at the morgue; you won't even have enough room. I'll hang your body upside down like a sheep at the butcher's and whip you so bad, when you report to the Lord on the Day of Judgment, he'll have difficulty recognizing you even when you show him your ID card."

Basile Okemba did thankless work. He was surrounded by the dead. Lifting those naked bodies, sticking them in drawers, was no ordinary job. He'd seen everything. Done everything. He'd shoveled up cadavers with a spade. He'd blocked up nostrils and ears that were oozing. Some dead bodies defecated several days after they were brought in. Others seemed to be grimacing, with their tongue sticking out. Others still had their jaws shut tight, as if they were terrified at the thought of passing from one world to the next. Worst of all was when he would patrol the great courtyard at midnight, a bulldog at his side. The windows of the hospital were closed. There was an icy silence. The trees seemed transfixed. Scrawny dogs rooted in the trash cans that were filled with dirty dressings. Basile Okemba would do the rounds of the hospital, a cigarette in his mouth. Shadows would pass in front of him. He didn't look at them. They were for sure stray souls who hadn't accepted that their time had come and that they needed to dissolve, to quit the bodies that had housed them. At that moment the bulldog, which was a few yards ahead of Basile Okemba, would give a bark.

You had to be a little bit mad to work at the morgue, some people said. Or a sorcerer, others added. It was during that time that Basile Okemba had acquired the habit of talking to himself. His words sounded disjointed to anyone who heard them.

He would talk to the dead. Hurl abuse at them, rail at them when one of their arms fell out of a drawer. The dead listened, obeyed him. When he came home in the evening, the smell of cadavers filled the place. Because of his profession, he had given up eating meat, he who had seen the human body from every angle.

As for Gaston's two brothers, their school days were worse than chaotic. The first failed his exams over and over again. The other kept having to repeat years and planned to learn cabinetmaking in the workshop of Mvoundou Joseph, a.k.a. Mompéro Mwana Mawa, the most highly regarded cabinetmaker in Pointe-Rouge. He specified that he would be a cabinetmaker but that he'd never make caskets. A joke that Basile Okemba did not much appreciate.

Gaston had become the sole source of support for the family, and he was a good provider. Later on, when he had to visit his family, he would never fail to take Christiane, who had been adopted at once by his brothers and his parents.

VII

Life in Pointe-Rouge

Christiane and Gaston's relationship took root. She moved out of the Post Office Workers Hostel, and they rented a house near the central market, the busiest point in the capital. I myself had never set foot there, and so I was always enthralled by Christiane's stories. Even that day of our farewell, when she revisited her memories, I'd imagined myself in that environment, teeming with people, cars, mopeds. I told myself that it was totally different from life in the North, where at six o'clock in the evening everything shuts down. Only Mapapouville, our political capital, could compete with Pointe-Rouge. The very first time when she'd disclosed her past to me so unrestrainedly, at our second meeting on that memorable Sunday, Christiane had been stunned by my ignorance on the subject of Pointe-Rouge. Abruptly she stopped braiding my hair, letting go of the porcupine quill she was using to separate the strands, which almost stabbed me. She put her hands on her hips and stared openmouthed in astonishment.

"No, that's not possible, I don't believe it!"

Then she spoke to me of the Avenue de l'Indépendance, of Félix-Éboué Circle, of the different neighborhoods—Rex, Fond, Tiétié, Roy, Voungou, Makayamakaya, Mbota, and so on. She recalled that they'd been happy living there, she and Gaston, in that city that had adopted them. They would go to the classiest cafés and discos in the capital. Gaston was familiar with every nook and cranny of the place. He claimed he knew it better than his home district in the North.

She cleared her throat and let out a deafening "yiiehh!"—her way of expressing her elation at the thought of those times.

I listened to her. She knew by heart the songs and the movies that had left their mark on Vietongo. The Vietongolese rumba held no secrets for her. And by the way, according to her, Gaston was the best dancer she'd ever known. You had to see him dance. She swore she was incapable of describing it. It was a thing unto itself. How could you convey the feints and the dribbling of our best soccer players, Paul Sayal Moukila for instance, when he entered the opposing team's penalty area? How could you portray the movements of old Mouboungoulou, the most gifted of our traditional dancers, when the tom-tom drummer, swept up in a trance, invented drumrolls that he had forgotten by the next morning? Gaston in action was a treat to look at. You'd have sworn he was levitating. He had an incomparable way of waving his body back and forth, then becoming one with his partner, and finally spinning on his own axis. It was at the time when the musician Pamelo Mounka had come back from France and was at the peak of his career, making the entire continent dance, even the white volunteers who were living in our country and who were sick of the Viennese waltzes with their set moves that had been in force for generations.

The men in those days wore *pountcha* pants, flared at the bottom, with Salamander shoes and coats with broad lapels and a single vent in back. There was also the abacost-safari, the local jacket, worn with a wrap or a Tergal, for those opposed to wearing Western clothes. The tailors of the city all knew how to make those jackets though Master Boger was the specialist. You could see him standing outside his workshop opposite the Vicky Photo Studio. Master Boger always had his scissors in his hand and a pencil in the pocket of his abacost. He sewed more than ten outfits a day with his apprentices, who he watched like a hawk. He was Gaston's tailor of choice.

Yet young people soon were making fun of this style, claiming such jackets were worn by the Téké, a Vietongolese tribe whose men had deep scarifications on their faces. These youngsters had renamed it the "Safari Muzaka Batéké," and in fact a popular song went:

> Safari Muzaka Batéké
> Eyayeh I do not know
> Ohé ohé balosa mu cabiné

On their feet people wore Salamanders. These shoes that came from France added at least four inches for men lacking in the height department! You needed to have them. You had to have them. Even the president in those times, the youngest in our history, was never seen without them—he who was the shortest president on the continent.

Christiane was adamant: elegance in men showed in many things. Such men had a sense of look, with their mustaches, their Afro hair, their pleated *pountcha* pants, their big leather belts with steel death's-head buckles. Their way of walking was inspired by Jim Kelly in *Three the Hard Way*, with Jim Brown and Fred Williamson, American actors of that time.

On that memorable Sunday Christiane had started on a big digression. She couldn't mention *Three the Hard Way* without elaborating for a few minutes. She told me that the images they'd seen in this film contrasted sharply with the Indian movies that were all over the country, whose endings were so easy to guess: the plot would boil down to the fact that the hero, who was always handsome and sexy, had to suffer torments before rejoining his lady love, at which point he would take his revenge on the evil creatures of hell.

Christiane and Gaston had seen one of these films at the Duo Cinema. As she told it, it was a day she would not forget quickly. One minute from the end of the film, the hero, the handsome, charming man that the audience was rooting for, was killed by a fearsome monster. Previously this creature had terrified the entire theater, breathing flames from its huge nostrils, to the point that elderly persons sitting in the front rows had had to beat a retreat before the end. The film caused an outcry. You could do anything, but you didn't have the right to kill the hero. The feeling of disappointment was universal. A funereal silence was followed by indignation. Sobs came from the back of the room. Discussion among the audience turned into arguments. Everyone was shouting, "We want our money back!" People smashed up the seats.

According to Christiane, it wasn't the first time the Duo had witnessed such discontent and material destruction. One afternoon, many years before, in the time of westerns, the audience there had given a half-hour standing ovation for a certain American actor by the name of Clint Eastwood, who in the final scene, at the crucial moment, had killed a mustachioed, potbellied, sombrero-clad bandit in a hail of bullets. The film was over, but the cheers and the hugging and kissing continued among the viewers. The theater could breathe again. The worst had been avoided. The villain had gotten on everyone's nerves with his sangfroid and his trigger-happy ways. He never missed. Many people had closed their eyes when the mustachioed man in the sombrero aimed his gun at the audience. He ruled the roost in a town where even the sheriff had turned in his star and decided to go raise horses in the mountains with his family. That bandit deserved to die. The theater, which was packed that day, was delighted by the film, by its ending, especially when they saw the mustachioed guy lying on the ground in a pool of blood, never to get up again. The tension dropped.

"Well done!"

"Take that, you louse!"

"We told you you were going to die, and now you see! Yes oh yes!"

Alas, this collective joy was clouded by an unusual circumstance for the regulars of the Duo: a second western came up on the program, starring the same bandit who'd been killed in the movie they'd seen two weeks before. He was again playing the villain, with even fancier weapons and a rapidity that the audience compared to that of Lucky Luke, the hero of comic books on sale on the sidewalk in front of the cinema, along with novels by Guy des Cars, San-Antonio, Georges Simenon, and Paul Kenny, and also magazines like *Hi Pals* and *Podium*, in which young people could find posters of their idols: Michel Sardou, Michel Polnareff, Dave, Claude François, and Sheila and Ringo as a couple.

"They really take us for idiots. Hey there!"

"That crook's still alive?"

"I thought he died two weeks ago?"

"Are you sure it's really him?"

"No, it's not him, it's some other guy. Take it easy. This one doesn't have a mustache or a hat."

"No, it really is him! They've cut off his mustache and taken away his hat so as to fool us! It's him! I recognize his gold tooth."

"Oh yes, you're right!"

"They've pulled a fast one on us!"

"Well I'm not going to stand for that, not me!"

"Give us our money back!"

And the audience left the theater in midscreening, swearing they'd never go to any more westerns because they were sick of the lies and the fakery.

According to Christiane, *Three the Hard Way* was, on the other hand, received in Pointe-Rouge as a film of quite another caliber, with splendid fights, payback, and the triumph of good over evil. With this movie a new page was definitively turned: the Pointe-Rouge viewers were dazzled to see that Blacks too could play starring roles in karate movies. The same viewers bore a grudge against martial arts movies like *Game of Death*, in which Bruce Lee had dared to administer a thrashing to Black actor Kareem Abdul-Jabbar. It was a disgrace! It was rigged! How could a Black man over seven feet tall like Kareem Abdul-Jabbar let himself be floored by a man who barely reached up to his navel?

With *Three the Hard Way*, these filmgoers recovered their pride, to the point of turning their backs on the big Indian films like *The Magician of Hell* or *Mandala, Daughter of India . . .*

The Demonstration

Who could have lived in Pointe-Rouge and not known the café-bar Les Rapides? Fine automobiles. Fine clothes. Show. The Mères ya Kilo, the Mama Benzes, these businesswomen who traveled to West Africa, knew how to knot their super-wax wrap dresses around their backs, which then swayed to the magical guitar rhythms of Master or of Jerry Gérard. Primus and Kronenbourg in collared bottles flowed abundantly. In a melancholy voice, Christiane began murmuring the words of "She's Only My Secretary," the hit by Pamelo Mounka from that year:

> Yesterday I was chatting with my secretary
> You saw us and you made a scene
> Bolingo na pesa epayi na yo
> Na koki kokabela ndambo mibalé té marna . . .
> Mam na bana
> Opusa jealousy oh oh
> You are my love
> Tika jealousy oh oh
> She's only my secretary
> There's nothing between us . . .

On that Sabbath, matching her actions to her words, with staccato movements Christiane performed a few steps of the famous makolo pente dance. Her legs stiffened, crossed, spread with the speed of an athlete. She squatted, then jumped up, while her head nodded, majestically tracing an invisible circle around her shoulders. With her eyes closed, she imagined a partner that she swept along with her. I couldn't stop her; we barely knew each other. The truth was that I myself was enchanted by her way of bringing this past back to life. Christiane seemed possessed by a spirit that dictated what to tell me. It all flowed with a clarity that gave substance to every fact. She murmured "Money Calls to Money," another hit by the same singer, who she appeared to venerate above all the other musicians of our country:

> Money calls to money
> Mbongo eko benga mbongo oooh
> Mbongo eko benga mbongo oooh
> It's only lent to the rich
> Never saw a rich man lend money to a poor man
> I go to the bank
> Where I'm a client
> To ask for credit
> Since I want to be rich
> But they make it hard for me
> Because I have no money
> Oh if I were rich
> There'd be no problem . . .

VIII

The Lady Postal Worker

The day of our farewell, Christiane was no longer the beautiful woman of that unforgettable long-ago Sunday. In her mind she must have found herself once again in the little two-room apartment that Gaston rented in the Rex neighborhood of Pointe-Rouge. How many times had she made the trip from her Post Office hostel to Rex, to see the man she couldn't be apart from anymore? It wasn't exactly easy for her—she lived on the other side of the city from that neighborhood, which she also needed to cross by public transportation each morning and evening on her way to and from work. On this journey she would imagine herself back in Batalébé; images from her childhood, and her successful application for a post office job, would come back to her in snatches. She never forgot that she'd been very young when she lost her father, at five years old. She only had a vague memory of him: a tall, thin man with a solemn voice that she would hear as she sat under a flame tree a few yards away from her parents, who were working in the fields. She would have wished that guardian shade to have been there on the day of her triumph. Her father would have been proud of her. He would have marched her around the district. But she'd known such happiness only with her mother. She'd just turned eighteen, and her older brother was already living in France. At the time she won the post office position, mail delivery involved primarily the big cities of the country. Out in the rural districts a mail carrier came by once a month on a bicycle. Each district had only one mail carrier, often the same one for decades. He could be seen growing old on his bicycle and refusing to pass the baton to the younger generation. Christiane was lucky to be appointed to Pointe-Rouge, which she had preferred over Mapapouville because she thought the latter was too far from Batalébé. That year, her admission into the post office was a big event in the district. She was the only one to be accepted, though all the parents had encouraged their children to apply. Christiane knew that the tests were tough. There was dictation, math, history, and above all geography. You had to be able to draw a map of Vietongo, know its different regions, its bodies of water, the size of the population and its distribution throughout the country. You had to learn by heart the capitals of most of the countries of the world. And physical education couldn't be neglected. Christiane had passed all these hurdles. Her success caused quite a stir in the district.

The Wandering Brother

She looked after her mother from Pointe-Rouge, sending her registered parcels, money, sacks of rice. She dreamed of returning to Batalébé, of working close to her mother, who was her only connection to family. After the death of her father, their relatives had scattered in a dismal story involving land and plantations. Since then the uncles, aunts, cousins, and other relations had gone their own ways. She could no longer count on the older brother whose name she didn't even want to pronounce, and who had lived for a time in Mapapouville before quitting that city for France. Ten years separated her from Léopold Mpassi-Mpassi. But they seemed to have nothing in common, not even blood; the brother loathed his little sister, convinced that their parents showed preference to her in every way. Christiane hadn't known him well. Her mother would tell her of the mischief Léopold Mpassi-Mpassi used to get up to in the district. Not a week went by without someone from Batalébé coming to complain about his behavior. The theft of fruit could at a pinch be forgiven. But he and the gangs of urchins from the center of town would go stealing sheep, pigs, poultry. His father, who might have been able to straighten out this waywardness, had gone to the other world.

They learned that, led by his friends to the cities of Vietongo from the age of fifteen, Léopold Mpassi-Mpassi was roaming the streets of Mapapouville, throwing himself into delinquency and thinking only of leaving to go abroad. The city had transformed him. He had passed through the various stages and had become an adult. He smoked cannabis in the streets and thumbed his nose at the police. Europe was in his sights, as was the case for many young people roaming the famous Bleu-Blanc-Rouge neighborhood of Mapapouville. No one had been informed about his departure for France. Léopold had preferred to sever all ties with the country, including with his sister and his mother. The latter no longer spoke about it, even when her daughter persisted in asking questions. She had lost her son from the moment he was born. Unlike Christiane, Léopold Mpassi-Mpassi had come out of her belly feet first, so as to test the terrain. The message sent by the little baby could not have been clearer: all his life he would do nothing but walk and wander, and he'd scoff at the conventions laid down by society.

IX

The Flow of Memories Interrupted

She was sweating. The sound of pigs walking upstream along the river cut into her journey into the past. She half opened her eyes. I was there, in front of her, saying nothing.

"What are you doing here?"

I didn't answer.

"Haven't you gone already?" she continued, rubbing her eyes. "I'm sorry, I've never stopped thinking about that Sunday when I told you my life story. So you've decided to leave Batalébé, that's it?"

I nodded.

"Back then, when I spoke to you about my life, about Pointe-Rouge, everything was so wonderful!"

"Yes," I agreed, clapping my hands together to kill an insect that was buzzing around her head.

"It's such a pity you never knew Pointe-Rouge. But I know you'll make it there, maybe you'll even live there."

The effort of memory had left furrows on her forehead. She brought the photograph close to her face and gave the faintest of smiles.

"You must go home now, Hortense. You've taken a risk in coming here this time. You could have left the district without seeing me, I wouldn't have held it against you. Go now . . ."

She leaned back against the wall, without letting go of the photograph. Her eyelids grew heavy again, then closed. This string of memories must have been overwhelming for her.

Yes, it was our last meeting, our day of farewell. Perhaps everything was jumbled in her mind. She was certain that I knew her life from beginning to end. I was virtually its guardian. I would have liked for us to talk for a long time, but a silence was parting us. I had let her slip away, follow the twists and turns of her recollections. We seemed to be communicating through our thoughts.

Final Return to Memories

I was no longer going to delay leaving her. On her face, with its closed eyes, I'd seen a sort of relief, a kind of serenity. But I sensed she would reread another few pages of her past, especially her appointment to Batalébé, which had come right after the death of her mother, when Gaston had set foot in Christiane's region for only the third time. The first had been to introduce her friend to her mother. The two women had talked aside for a moment, the mother wanting to know more about the man who was to become her son-in-law. The second time was to announce the marriage, which was going to take place six months later in Pointe-Rouge, where they tied the knot among a small circle of friends and coworkers. Gaston's family had been there. Christiane's mother had not made the trip, despite the urging of the future couple. She had, wrongly, been wary of the city, about which she'd heard so many bad things that she was convinced she'd be attacked by bandits on her way there. Plus, when she imagined the long journey all the way to Pointe-Rouge, she was reinforced in her decision not to leave Batalébé for anything in the world. Indeed, she would have had to cross the South in a truck overloaded with goods and passengers. Each run was fraught with danger. The bridges usually unnerved those traveling for the first time, whenever they arrived at a river. These bridges, which had been constructed by hand by the local population, all resembled one another: two large tree trunks joining the two banks of the river. The trucks had to keep their tires on them as they crossed. The driver's aide would ask if anyone wished to get out and cross to the other side on foot using one of the trunks, arms spread like a tightrope walker on a rope. Dizziness was a constant possibility. But no one chose to leave the vehicle, for fear of losing their seat once they'd crossed the river. This meant that the truck was even heavier, more prone to tragedy. The only ones who got down were the intrepid folks perched on the covered top of the truck. As for the drivers, they were used to this perilous exercise. They operated the steering wheel nimbly, and once they felt the vehicle's center of gravity on the bridge, they stepped on the gas. One false move and the travelers would all end up at the bottom of the river. That had happened several times in the region. When it did, people said that the spirits of the river, the *Mami Wata*, had called for a sacrifice for the purpose of regulating the waters, to avoid an unprecedented flood in the region.

The Funeral of Mother Kengué

The third time Gaston had come to Batalébé was for the funeral of his mother-in-law, who had died of malaria in the middle of the night, in the same remote house that Christiane would inherit and in which they were going to live.

How could she fail to recall her mother's funeral? All of Batalébé had been there, except for the district chief, who had delegated one of his deputies. Gaston and his family formed a group apart. Not knowing anyone, they found it hard to understand this world, which expressed itself in the multiple languages of the South. Word had quickly gotten around that Gaston was the husband of Christiane and that he was from the North. Many people came to greet him. Others eyed him from a distance without hiding their curiosity. Gaston kept his eyes glued on his wife, who was surrounded by the elderly women of the district, many of whom had been childhood friends of the deceased. Christiane wore a black scarf that covered her face. From time to time one of the old ladies brought her water or coffee to drink, but the rites of her tribe called on her to avoid eating in public and to stay away from her husband. The wake lasted three days and three nights. On the day of the interment, to the general satisfaction, the sky donned its most somber vestments, thunder sounded, and it rained profusely: that is how the dead of Batalébé take their leave from those who remain here below. The rain is said to wash away the bad things they have done without meaning to, so the gates of Eternity will open for them.

The district accompanied the body all the way to its final resting place in the Mampembé Cemetery, a few hundred yards from the deceased's house. The elderly women remained three more days to stand vigil over the grave, then went their own ways, folding away their bedrolls. Madame Kengué now lay by her husband, close to their home and to Christiane.

Léopold Mpassi-Mpassi did not get in touch.

Return to the Fold

After her mother's funeral, Christiane finally received her posting to Batalébé. She was appointed to a post office that had just been created by the Postal and Telecommunications Ministry as part of the national campaign to "open up the back country." At this time every district was given a post office, often built of planks, with a used vehicle that had to be pushed by passersby whenever it got stuck in the mud.

At first Christiane had come to Batalébé alone. She seemed a little disoriented, but she wanted to live close to her mother's grave, and that of her father, who, it seems, had been taken by the same illness as that which had ended her mother's life. The latter hadn't had the chance to get to know Gaston better. All she knew was that he was from far away. From the North. That had been enough to put her on her guard. She felt duty bound to warn her daughter about the dangers of such a union. She took her aside on the first day Christiane had introduced the northerner. Madame Kengué spoke to her daughter, looking her straight in the eye to make sure she'd thought hard before choosing a man who came from more than six hundred miles from their district and who did not understand most of the languages of the South. Christiane burst out laughing and did not answer her mother.

The second question only came later. Simply because the mother was afraid of her daughter's reaction. Madame Kengué took the plunge: "Tell me the truth: he beats you, this northerner ..."

Like everyone in Batalébé, she was convinced that northerners were nothing but barbarians, brutes, jealous creatures who spent their time beating their wives like dusty carpets.

Christiane replied calmly: "Gaston has never so much as slapped me. I, on the other hand, gave him a slap one time, and I regret it ..."

"What? And he didn't do anything to you afterwards?"

"No."

Madame Kengué was speechless with incredulity.

Christiane gazed at her fixedly and added: "That man wouldn't hurt a fly ..."

That day Madame Kengué put her arms around Gaston as if he'd been her own child. She had just understood that from this point on her daughter was the only person who mattered to her. She no longer thought of Léopold Mpassi-Mpassi, the ungrateful son who looked very much like her late husband. He had the same features. Léopold Mpassi-Mpassi had been a strange child who was always staring at the horizon, as if he were plotting within himself the route he would take when the wings of Liberty grew on his back. He rarely opened his mouth, and until he was five years old, they'd thought he would not speak. In fact he heard all words, all sounds. Then one day, to everyone's surprise, he'd opened his mouth. First to repeat the word "No!" several times and refuse to eat. Then to let out a series of hysterical howls, after which he beat his chest like a gorilla. The abuse he spouted exasperated his parents, and the hidings he received did not deter him from such behavior. He had directed an inexplicable hatred against his sister from the moment she was born. Léopold Mpassi-Mpassi could not comprehend the arrival of this tiny being that was dependent on their mother's breasts and that enjoyed the attention, all the attention, of their parents. He was caught over and over spitting on his little sister or trying to smother her. After that the mother or the father always made sure to be close by. The brother and sister had grown up like this, in an atmosphere of conflict that the father had in his lifetime been unable to dispel.

A Rock in Place of a Heart

Léopold Mpassi-Mpassi was so resilient that his schoolteachers said it was useless to cane him in class for a bad grade—you never heard him cry like his classmates, who would be sobbing before the cane even struck their calves. This trait got worse as he grew older. A withdrawn, secretive boy, he gave his mother a headache by spiriting away her savings, even though she kept them hidden in her locked bedroom. When his mother spoke to him, the boy got mad, threw rocks at her, and then went to sleep in the market square with the stray dogs of the district. Then

Madame Kengué, who by that time was already a widow, threw in the towel; the teenager became even tougher in character and grew ever nastier. He was from a different world. Perhaps she told herself that life had not been easy on her. She seemed to spend her life atoning for sins she hadn't committed. Fate had taken away her husband and left her with two children of twelve and five. In the middle of his teenage years, the son with the nasty disposition had slipped out of the district and set off in a truck for Mapapouville in search of adventure. She had cried, but she ran out of tears because her son never came back home again. She loved him, that son of hers, despite his abominable behavior. She virtually wore mourning for him, up to the moment when she learned he'd been terrorizing the elderly in the Bleu-Blanc-Rouge neighborhood. Léopold Mpassi-Mpassi had descended into delinquency. At the head of some gang of young hooligans or other, he plagued the poorly lit quarters of Mapapouville. Madame Kengué only breathed easier when the young man went to France: people said only good things about that country. France would temper the young rebel's activities. He couldn't have continued his bad-boy behavior in that land of snow. From France his mother received a letter, or rather a scrap of paper. It was the only document that linked her to her son. "I'm never coming back," Léopold Mpassi-Mpassi had written. He was living in the twelfth arrondissement, on the rue du Congo. That was it; there were no other details.

After the death of her mother, the letter came into Christiane's possession; she too had reread it from time to time, when the image of the vagabond of Mapapouville haunted her thoughts. She would imagine her brother on the street that bore the name of a country in this continent: rue du Congo. The piece of paper had faded. A long time ago, Madame Kengué used to unfold it, study her son's hesitant yet vigorous handwriting. If it hadn't been for the stamp saying "République Française," she wouldn't have believed her son really lived in France, with an address like that. She'd often predicted she would die without seeing again that neglectful son, who could not be bothered to make the journey even when he received the news. He had a rock in place of a heart; no doctor could have operated on him to give him a real heart, a human heart.

She had not been mistaken.

Gaston Arrives in Batalébé

Gaston rejoined his wife in Batalébé two months after she herself had settled in. He'd been transferred to a local branch of the National Office of Public Works that covered the districts of Batalébé, Komono, Ndounga, and Tsiaki. He traveled constantly among these places. His office was located between Batalébé and Komono. In fact, he and his colleagues were responsible for overseeing the famous Moukoukoulou Dam, one of the last gifts of China to the Vietongolese people: a token of friendship between nations that advocated "government of the people, by the people, for the people and the people alone." The dam was strategically important in the country. It provided drinking water, produced energy for a good part of Vietongo and also for neighboring countries. On top of which, it irrigated farms throughout the South.

Christiane gradually got used to the public works jargon that at the beginning Gaston would parrot as he sought to practice on her. In his frequent flights of technical speech, at the table, even on Sundays, he would speak in minute detail of the different kinds of dams, as if he'd attended Bridges and Roads—a school, he said, that was respected by the Whites themselves, and that kept cropping up in his talk ever since he'd taken his new position. He would elucidate, for example, that a rock-fill dam was a structure made of loose rocks and that its stability depended entirely on the watertightness of the upstream face. That had to be understood. He would add that a gravity dam usually had a triangular shape and resisted the current by its weight alone. Here too, he himself was figuring out the things he was saying. All of this to explain to Christiane that the huge structure of Moukoukoulou was rather an arch dam. A triumph of engineering, the concrete barrage directed the pressure of the water onto the banks by its arched form, and it had a convex curvature facing upstream.

Christiane had been intrigued, and one day she paid a visit. The whole thing looked like a flying saucer that had fallen in the middle of the river and was holding back the water to the level of the trees on the banks. Gaston was pleased by her visit. He spent hours elaborating the details of the dam and telling her legends that he'd heard along the Moukoukoulou River since he'd taken up his post.

The Inherited House

The couple restored the Batalébé house that Christiane had just inherited from her mother. The straw roof was replaced by aluminum sheeting. Christiane had especially wanted to put her Singer sewing machine near the window that she opened in the morning. The daylight entered the house and lit up the symbol of their love. Without that Singer, which of the two of them would have made the first move?

The house in Batalébé came back to life, with a little garden in back and the end of the plot marked by the mango trees that blossomed in September. Their home was far from the center, and it was rare that anyone ventured near. Christiane would go into town, especially on market days.

The district chief, a bald, potbellied little man in glasses with a nasal voice, paid the couple a visit one day. He offered his apologies for not having been present at the funeral. He was sorry about Madame Kengué, who had joined her husband in the cemetery.

"They were decent people who loved the district and who embodied its deepest values. Life is so blind that it usually only cuts down those who still have some ideal to transmit; let me assure you, your parents-in-law were of that stamp."

Always that pompous official tone, thought Christiane.

The chief claimed to be glad that a compatriot from the North had chosen to settle in a small place in the South.

"Naturally, reasons of the heart often prevail in one's decisions, whatever they may be," he had proclaimed when he had gotten up and, in the company of his two bodyguards, headed for the black Peugeot 405 waiting for him out front.

"Remember that I'll always be here. Don't hesitate to get in touch whenever you wish. It would be a pleasure."

* * *

At that point Kimbembé and I were just leaving the Oweto district in the North for Batalébé. It was also the first time I had set foot in the South of Vietongo, far from my native region. Maribé had been in my belly for four months.

The Reminiscences Come to an End
A Farewell Gift

I was now sure that Christiane's journey into the past had come to an end. She opened her eyes. I was afraid she would ask me the same questions as she had each time she came back to reality. I sat there, still not saying anything.

At no point had Christiane let go of the photograph, which she was still holding tight to her chest. She looked me in the eye, perhaps waiting for me to ask her what she had been thinking about in the sort of dead time during which we could hear the wingbeat of the flies.

She was fully aware that I had figured everything out. It had been enough for me to see the sweat trickling down her forehead to let me imagine her inner dialogue. Moments of joy made her nostrils flare. Surprise made her perk up her ears. Frustration caused her mouth to contract. Reflection made her lift her chin. I had been noting these details attentively. That was how I'd been able to accompany her as a discreet witness during the ups and downs of her reverie.

Christiane seemed worn out, defenseless, out of breath, her top soaked with perspiration. The question I had been dreading came out of her mouth at the moment I least expected it:

"Have you not gone home yet?"

"No," I replied. "What are our chances of getting away from the Negro Grandsons?"

In the face of her silence and her barely open eyes, I took the last nuts from the bowl and ate them without appetite.

Night had fallen on Batalébé. Yet it was hard for me to leave her. She reminded me that it was the last time we'd see each other.

"I don't think so," I said unconvincingly.

"You know it, things like that can be felt. It would be easier for two of Vietongo's mountains to meet each other than for the two of us, except in the next world. But I'll be there before you," she concluded, looking toward the cemetery where her parents were at rest.

A silence followed her words. I was still sitting. Out of habit I let her take the lead in permitting me to go. She pointed out again that my daughter was at home and that I ought to hurry back to take care of her.

She asked me to get up. She put the photo on the little table and lit a hurricane lamp whose glass was dirtied with smoke.

A flickering light encircled our two faces, while the rest of the house was plunged in shadow.

"You have to leave now; your daughter's waiting for you, and tomorrow is a big day for the two of you. All I can do is wish you both luck. Walk on, don't give in to despondency or fear. Remember to take a radio, that's important. I'll never forget you, Hortense. You're more than a friend to me. Take good care of your daughter."

She put her arms around me.

Our embrace went on and on. Neither of us wanted it to end. She was sobbing, and I couldn't help doing so too.

She pulled away from me, turned around, and scratched her head, thinking hard about something. Finally making up her mind, she moved back to the rickety table, returned with the photograph, and kissed me. She showed me the picture again. Did she wish me to look at it one last time so as to fix her existence forever in my memory? She held it out toward me like a trophy. I didn't understand what she wanted of me.

"Keep it with you. That way we'll always be by your side."

"No, Christiane, it's the only photo you have of the two of you . . ."

"Do it for me, Hortense. Take the picture with you when you leave. Go on, have it, here."

A last glance at the image that was now in my hands: the couple seemed to be sadder. Even Gaston's smile appeared to have faded. I no longer recognized the faces. Maybe in the morning, with the sunrise, the brightness of their life would break the glass protecting them, I said to myself. Then I'd see Gaston smile again, see Christiane with her affected yet touching expression. All of that I'd see only by the light of day, or probably never. We were about to slip away from the district.

Parting

As I left Christiane I was thinking only of the name of the village stuck in my head: Louboulou. I turned the photograph over and found a folded scrap of paper wedged in the corner of the frame. I took it out carefully and read aloud in a low voice:

> I'm never coming back
> Rue du Congo, 75012 Paris
> Léo...

It was the curt letter that Léopold Mpassi-Mpassi had sent long ago to Madame Kengué.

PART TWO
FROM OWETO IN THE NORTH TO
BATALÉBÉ IN THE SOUTH

I

Louboulou, Place of Transit

Round houses of baked clay or packed earth. Crumbling walls that make it seem as if people are watching you from inside. From time to time a skinny, wary farm animal crosses the only road, which cuts the village in two. The creature stretches, opens its jaws wide to express simultaneously its hunger, its boredom, and its despair. It turns on its own axis as if it were overcome by dizziness, before stretching out behind a madder bush . . .

Louboulou is an expanse of red earth surrounded by hills, with an ill-sorted collection of houses each far from the next. The trash littering the main square put us off from the moment of our arrival. Most of the house roofs have been torn open by the winds of the dry season. Animal carcasses lie about on the ground, eyed by vultures. The vegetation is covered in yellow dust. The stooping trees wave their frail branches that brush against the earth, their leaves scorched by the sun. The horizon comes to an end toward the last houses of the village. Every evening the sun, more interested in pursuing its round elsewhere, scrapes the thatched roofs before it disappears waveringly over the top of one of the region's ancient baobab trees . . .

Arrival in Louboulou

We arrived here at the end of the day. We had gotten a little lost moving away from the river where we'd stopped to eat.

Southerners usually build their villages near flowing water, and we had told ourselves that all we had to do was follow the river and we'd run into Louboulou. Yet we did the opposite, taking other paths that led into the bush. Exhausted as we were, we found ourselves back at the place where we'd stopped at midday and where I had seen the shadow of Kimbembé in military uniform.

The river was in front of us again.

We followed it all afternoon and grew familiar with the way it behaved. It broadened, narrowed, muttered, calmed itself, divided, joined other branches. In taking this way we had stayed far from the highway where the Negro Grandsons of Vercingetorix might come by in their jeeps. Even from a helicopter it would be impossible to spot us under the dense vegetation.

Toward evening we thought we heard another river murmuring nearby. We told ourselves it must be a branch of the one we were following. In fact it was another stream that emerged from a massive boulder. The water appeared sky blue and transparent by turns. Not far from that place, we noticed mounds of earth with crosses.

A cemetery.

So we were on the banks of Crayfish Creek, close to Louboulou!

After walking a few more minutes, we saw the first houses.

Passing the cemetery, we went toward the main square, in the middle of which was a tumbledown clapboard building. It was the only structure with a proper four-sided roof. I put down the bundle I had been carrying on my back. Maribé sat down at my feet, and we looked around as if we were waiting for someone to come greet us . . .

First Impressions

The rural exodus has been merciless here. You'd think that the last remaining inhabitants were hoping only for fate to transport them to the next world. Then the village would pass away, vanish forever from the map of Vietongo. Nothing would be left but a vague memory strung on a leafy branch of one of the old local baobabs. Any pilgrim venturing into this region would imagine regretfully that life had once flourished in it, upon discovering here a canary lying in the mud, there the hollow gourd of a palm-wine tapper, or elsewhere the shaft of a miniature hoe whose rusted blade was buried somewhere in the layers of dry earth. Coming down the hill by Crayfish Creek, which had since time immemorial quenched the thirst of the inhabitants, our pilgrim would soon catch sight of the Louboulou Cemetery: mounds of earth, each topped with a cross fashioned from branches of acacia tied together with creepers. There are no inscriptions on the graves because here there's no need to name the dead. There's no need to tell them apart, to identify them. Never mind the confusion: the dead are able to return to the reality of things among themselves. So then, on the graves our pilgrim would perhaps be astonished to see aluminum plates, hurricane lamps, statuettes, bars of soap, shoes, hats, pipes, tobacco, and other objects that would enable the deceased to scale the mountains of the beyond and then rest in peace as they wait for the Day of Judgment. Southerners believe that death is not the end of the soul. Kimbembé used to remind me of that. The people of Louboulou knew it. For them death was merely a passage into the next world, the world of Eternity.

In the North, in my native region, we had the same notion, true, but we identified our dead clearly. You could read the deceased's date of birth and death. Many took their beliefs so far as to bury their loved ones in front of their own house, or even inside, keeping the spirit of the dead close so that they could continue to watch over them. In the North just as in the South, dying was the noblest of deliverances. In the South you don't die; you leave this world for the next. You reunite with your ancestors, who wait tranquilly for the members of the family to come together again in a single house and recall their former life, though without regrets. Yet not all deaths open the gates to eternal rest. Anyone who died a natural or accidental death can sit down at table with their ancestors, who will make room for them without hesitation. Whereas someone who put an end to their days by rope, knife, or any other means would be subject to the wrath of the ancestors for all time. Driven from any assembly in the hereafter, they would come back to wander the earth. And phantom dogs would be at their heels. The barking of these creatures would prevent them from sleeping even for a moment.

In the South, the elders tell young people that they've seen the dead roaming the forest, behind the houses or along the rivers, because there was no room for them in the other world, where strait is the gate. So-and-so hanged himself, he was quickly buried, but you see him always at night, in tears, at the entrance to the village, not far from the cemetery, a rope around his neck.

II

Our Daily Life in Louboulou

Everything here seems frozen, suspended.

Birds with somber plumage cast a dismal shadow over the tops of the rows of Palmyra palms that enclose the houses. Their song travels across the hill, goes as far as the forest, and comes back in a crackling, fitful echo all the way to the first dwellings of the village. The buildings rise up in the immobility of a land laid low by a plague from which the inhabitants have been unable to recover and so have decided to give up the struggle. The kind of plague that above all should not be named, in case that should bring it back. So it's unsurprising that the scars of fate, the fissures of resignation, should be visible on the bark of the trees. Old people are rarely even seen poking their nose out of doors. The moment they appear, they hurry out to gather their chickens and livestock, then shut the door of their house behind them.

We live here, Maribé and I, opposite what once must have been the market square, in this abandoned house that belongs to Mam'Soko, the old lady suffering from chronic rheumatism. She was the one who came out to see us. She'd spotted us in the distance when we first arrived. She must have asked herself what a woman and a teenage girl could be looking for in a backwater like Louboulou. She must also have dug in her memory to see if we might not belong to some family in the village. She'd started to observe us from the moment we put our things on the ground.

* * *

In Louboulou Maribé sleeps a lot.

Her sleep is deep but still interspersed with delirium, with twitchings and sobbings. Mam'Soko always comes and knocks at the window. Yesterday she dropped off some kitchen utensils. She told us to make ourselves at home here and said we shouldn't hesitate to bother her if we needed anything. She told me again I should go out, take a walk with Maribé. I replied in the same way: we're tired and we want to rest. I turned on the radio to listen to the news. Reception was a little fuzzy, but the Voice of the Vietongolese Revolution could be heard clearly.

Mam'Soko went back into her orchard, a few of the animals that have remained loyal to her following in single file. She spent the day sitting under her tree, talking to it, stroking its fissured trunk. Then she got up and moved toward her house. She only half-closed the door. She didn't light her hurricane lamp. She waited for the shade of her husband. That's why she doesn't close the door. She prepared her rheumatism medication. You never know what might happen in the middle of the night. Before going to sleep, she chewed some tobacco leaves. Finally she lay down on her pallet and talked for a long time, until her eyelids grew heavy.

We didn't see her again till sunrise the next day . . .

Mam'Soko's Hospitality

A few days ago, when Mam'Soko first saw us standing in front of her second house, our belongings on the ground, she opened the door of her own house that was opposite it. I showed Maribé that someone was watching us. Night was slowly falling. We wondered whether we should go into the house or toward the old lady. The other inhabitants we'd seen did not seem at all surprised by our presence. Most of them were elderly. Some had walked by us without a glance. Others had given a slight nod and continued on their way.

Louboulou used to have a tradition of hospitality, especially at the time of well-fed cows, the shining years, when Massengo was alive. When travelers arrived in the evening, the villagers would slaughter a pig in their honor, offer them one of the houses for guests. Mam'Soko herself had opened the door of her second house wide. She had come forward with her stooping form, her hand gripping her cane. As she walked she mumbled unintelligible words, spitting on the ground. She came to a stop, trying in vain to straighten her back. Without a word she passed in front of us and opened the door of this second house of hers. We hesitated for a moment.

"This house has always welcomed strangers," she said. "Make yourselves at home here. The house belonged to my brother-in-law, who's in the cemetery at Crayfish Creek. Many people have slept here."

Inside the house the old lady pointed to a hurricane lamp in the corner. We lit it—night had fallen by now. Mam'Soko took the lamp in her trembling hand. She first brought it close to Maribé's face, which she scrutinized for a moment. Then she came up to me. At this point the light allowed me to see her features close up: dull, damp, yet mobile eyes; hollow cheeks; skin covered in wrinkles; thin ashen hair that barely covered part of her head. She sat on the ground as we unpacked our things. And she spoke about the village, about her husband, whose disappearance had remained in the collective memory . . .

* * *

Mam'Soko is from another era. Time has marked her. Her thinning hair has grown scorched as it turned white. She has had a life here. She reminded us that at one time Louboulou had a soul, had life. There were men, women, children. The dead wandered through the bushes, reincarnated as wild or domestic animals. That's the reason she steers clear of game, for fear of eating one of her loved ones, perhaps even her husband, whose death however she has never accepted. Yet Massengo died over twenty years ago. Mam'Soko cannot bring herself to accept his death because it was stranger than any other passing in Louboulou.

The Mysterious Story of Massengo the Hunter

Chief Massengo, Mam'Soko's husband, was an important person in the village. She speaks of him in the present tense even though he is dead. I have trouble acting as if he were still alive. At times, though, I find myself talking of him in the present, so as to respect Mam'Soko's world.

Though dead, Massengo is the chief of Louboulou. He is its mind, its breath, its soul. He left vast fields of cassava, banana plantations, and cattle. He was a hunter, one who never came home empty-handed. He could not have accepted such a shameful thing. He was a man with a sense of honor. He had left the village while defending it with all his strength. He had seen its end coming. Village chiefs are like gods: they know the date they will go away, but they tell no one, so as not to incur the wrath of the spirits.

Like all village chiefs, then, Massengo saw when his day came. Mam'Soko had in fact tried to persuade him not to go hunting that evening. Massengo, who was obstinate, claimed his instinct had told him that that night he would bag some big game, the biggest of his career. Armed with his 12mm, he left the village late at night. Mam'Soko saw him walk away and merge into the shadows.

The rain would not have put Massengo off. It's when the elements rage that a hunter achieves great things. Massengo encountered game leaping every which way in search of shelter among the branches.

It was the sorcerer Tongotsia who had retraced Massengo's story, watching the drama in a basin of clear water. The sorcerer explained to the wise ones of Louboulou that Chief Massengo had gotten lost in the bush and had found himself a long way from his region. He had been tracking some game. Game that he saw more in his head than in reality. The chief had kept walking, parting the branches, without ever once looking behind him. The rain fell. Thunder rolled, flattening trees. Massengo came out into a clearing. A blinding light had drawn him to this place, where the wind was gathering strength before unleashing its devastating fury. Massengo realized that his legs were buckling. That something was moving in front of him, coming toward him. The figure of an animal. A doe. The chief instinctively pulled the trigger.

A shot rang out. The recoil threw Massengo several yards away from the creature. Pulling himself together, he got back to his feet. He felt as if he were emerging from a long sleep. He picked up his gun, went up to the dead animal. His heart skipped a beat. The beast was still in its death throes. But that was not what puzzled him the most. What sent him mad was seeing that the animal had a human head. And not just any human head: that of Massengo, the hunter, the village chief himself . . .

That night Massengo had killed his own totem, the animal that was his double and that had been protecting him since he was born. Nothing could be done. This was how most village chiefs died in the South of Vietongo. They themselves killed their own double.

That was the explanation Tongotsia the sorcerer gave to the village. The body of the chief was recovered from the forest. There was no game by his side. His body was disfigured as if he had died by shooting himself in the head.

Mam'Soko and the Events

Mam'Soko is a little hard of hearing. Despite my explanations, she's not going to be able to understand why we're here. When I listen to the radio she seems surprised. She must not grasp any of it. She watches my thumb and forefinger as they turn the big dial to find the Voice of the Vietongolese Revolution.

The old lady thinks we've been thrown out by my husband; she assures me that in her day men acted the same. You just need to find some common ground, to talk with one another. Leaving is not a good way out.

I once asked her if she was aware of what was going on in Mapapouville these days. She didn't reply. She merely pointed out that I spoke Bembé with a marked northern accent.

Most often it's my daughter who repeats my words to her. Maribé puts her mouth right up to the old lady's ear and shouts. We've explained to her that I'm from the North, that I married a man from the South, and that we will have to leave for Pointe-Rouge in the coming days. She murmured something, and Maribé translated that she hadn't gotten any of what I'd told her.

I have the sense that after she's visited us she goes away with a ray of light on her forehead. She takes us for her daughters, she who never brought any children into the world. She claims that Maribé looks like me and that she would have liked to have a little girl like her. Each time we make food, I ask Maribé to take her a plate. Mam'Soko likes that.

In recent days she's even been bringing the plate back so she can eat with us. I took advantage of her being here to remind her that we'd be leaving very soon to head toward the Mayombe region, then one day continue on to Pointe-Rouge, which has been less affected by the events.

"What events?"

Her astonishment seemed so natural that I didn't say any more. She peered at my feet and Maribé's. Pointe-Rouge was several hundred miles from Louboulou. I told the old lady that our minds were made up. We'd walk, and when we found the railroad tracks, we'd follow them all the way to the end. She asked if we were going to take the train. I almost smiled, because I know now that there are no more trains. Trucks and cars are looted by the Negro Grandsons of Vercingetorix. The railroad that links Pointe-Rouge and Mapapouville is in such a bad state that to get it back in working shape, you'd need to mortgage all the oil wells of Vietongo present and future, to the profit of foreign oil companies. There were no more trains. The former stations had been turned into headquarters or bandit dens.

"We're going to walk," I insisted.

I didn't think the old lady placed any importance on what I said.

"You can have this house, Daughter. Do you not feel comfortable here?"

"Mother, we have to leave. I'm from the same region as General Edou . . ."

"Who's General Edou?" she replied in the same composed tone as when I'd spoken of the events in Mapapouville.

"Yes, Mother, General Edou."

I realized we could not talk of this.

The Rains

For the moment we're not leaving Louboulou. It's been raining a great deal recently. It would be risky to head out again into the bush, with rivers flooding and trees knocked down by the wind. We have to wait. Wait for the end of the rains. Wait for the rivers to settle. For the earth to become firm again. It'll take another week, ten days at the most. I think we'll slip out of Louboulou without telling Mam'Soko. That way our stay in this village will remain a mystery to her. She'll say we were nothing but passing shadows. Perhaps shadows from the world in which she's taken refuge.

The image of Christiane is still present. But I try to keep it at bay, to think about the rest of the journey that we'll make once circumstances permit. I refrain at all costs from talking about the situation in Mapapouville with my daughter, from mentioning the name of her father, Kimbembé, much less that of Vercingetorix. I let her listen to the Voice of the Vietongolese Revolution. Military songs all day long. Speeches by General Edou.

I feel somewhat guilty at having involved Maribé in this affair. Yet I'm convinced she knows that we could no longer endure our situation back in Batalébé. Admittedly, at seventeen she deserves a different existence from this one. A future other than fleeing her native region. That's partly why she didn't utter a word of protest before following me. I even had the impression that it was exactly what she had expected, and that my decision was late in coming.

IV

Maribé and Her Father

I can't claim that Maribé has always felt hatred toward her father. I think she rather came to her feelings once she realized she was no longer the little angel that Kimbembé would kneel before in the mornings. As if she'd been weaned prematurely. She reacted to this disregard with a fierce aggressiveness that took me by surprise. She even went so far as to believe that I was the reason they were no longer close. At those moments I would have liked to know what was going on in that adolescent brain of hers. She wasn't capable of evaluating the situation clearly. What mattered to her was that she remain the eighth wonder of the world to her father.

In fact, over time Kimbembé had changed a great deal. Was he even aware of Maribé's existence? He only ever came home in the middle of the night; without eating anything, he would head for the bedroom, from which fifteen minutes later we'd hear him snoring. He wouldn't utter a word about why he'd returned so late. What excuse could he offer, since lessons at the Jean-Malonga high school ended at five in the afternoon? The expression on his face dissuaded me from questioning him about his new ways. Frowning, his jaw set, his eyes cold and evasive, he'd drop his satchel on the floor and not say a word to anyone. Maribé in turn, imitating her father, would shut herself in her room. By way of revenge, she would not do her homework and would barely answer when I spoke to her.

This atmosphere contrasted sharply with the time when her relationship with her father was looking rosy. Actually, everything started to go to pot five years ago. Maribé had just turned twelve. If memory serves well, this goes back to our twelfth year in Batalébé. Up until then Kimbembé had pampered his daughter, made a fuss over her, to the point that I sometimes felt a certain jealousy, which I tried to suppress. Maribé saw me as a rival. This complicity between father and daughter had been going on a long time. Even at three months Maribé would only fall asleep when lying on her father's chest. It was in vain that I counted on the natural attachment all children are supposed to feel for their mothers, who have carried them for nine months in their belly; she preferred to listen to her father's heart beating, to stretch her little baby body out on Kimbembé, assured by a presence that made her feel safe.

A Difficult Birth

Christiane reckoned that my daughter's reaction was connected with the circumstances of her arrival in the world. Though I disagreed with her at the time, today I admit my friend from Batalébé was right.

In fact, in her view my husband was the cause of it all because, in contrast to other Vietongolese men, Kimbembé had insisted on being present at Maribé's birth in the Batalébé hospital. This was unthinkable in Vietongo. His friends, his fellow teachers at the Jean-Malonga High School, had treated him like a crazy person, a sadist, a sexual deviant. They were unanimous: how could anyone allow themselves to watch a child coming out of their wife's sex and then dare to touch her afterward? These were things that ought to remain veiled in mystery. Watch your own spouse give birth? Only Whites were capable of such madness, they had concluded at the time.

Kimbembé trampled on such taboos. He had waited for that moment, watching me as I slept during my pregnancy. The slightest cough alarmed him—he would think my time had come. He himself demanded to be in the delivery room. This request irked the Batalébé midwife. Such a thing had never happened in all the quarter of a century she'd been practicing. Usually men would drop their wives at the hospital entrance, then skedaddle. They'd go back home and wait for the event to happen. On top of that, after the child was born there was an interim period. The man didn't dare hold his baby till three months had passed. The woman stopped preparing meals and slept apart from her husband. A female cousin would take over the domestic duties.

In the face of unyielding opposition from the midwife, who refused to work in the presence of a man—one who was more-over the husband of the woman giving birth—Kimbembé wrote a letter to the director of the hospital, copying the provincial governor and the ministers of Health and of Social Services. This bold move outraged the hospital personnel, who stood behind their colleague the midwife. Rumors of a wildcat strike circulated in the hallways of the place. Kimbembé was considered a conceited young man who acted like a White. We'd been in Batalébé five months. Even though we were living in his native region, in those days Kimbembé was seen as an outsider. In fact our things were still up North, at my parents' place. To the hospital too we were nothing but strangers spreading our perversions among the peaceable inhabitants of Batalébé . . .

The Compromise

Two weeks before the due date, Kimbembé finally got the consent of the hospital director, after the governor and the two ministers had responded favorably to his letter. Cheered, my husband waved this correspondence in the midwife's face; yet she was not placated.

She snapped back: "The governor and the ministers can send another midwife. *I'm not going in there!*"

The director of the hospital had to tread a fine line. In the last days before the birth, a compromise was reached: Kimbembé would remain in the delivery room during the preliminary phase. Once the preparations were well advanced and the contractions more frequent, he would leave and wait in a nearby room. The midwife and two colleagues would proceed with my delivery.

Kimbembé accepted this solution, willingly or otherwise. In any case, he submitted to the decision. He put on light-blue overalls, which the embittered assistants of the midwife flung his way.

And that was how he came to take some part in our daughter's birth.

Maribé arrived. And soon a complicity between father and daughter would also be born.

Maribé's Education

Kimbembé followed little Maribé's every step. He was an attentive father concerned for the education of his daughter. In the evening when he came back from work, he would always ask the same questions:

"Where's Maribé?"

"In her room," I'd reply.

"Has she eaten?"

"Yes."

"What did she eat?"

And the same questions would be asked the following day.

Kimbembé took his daughter's education seriously. As well as certain texts from French literature, such as the fables of La Fontaine and Florian, he read her *Tales of the Bush and the Forest*. Then later, along with other children of her age, she learned to read and write from *Le Petit Syllabaire*, the textbooks of the African and Madagascaran Pedagogical Institute, which were referred to according to level, as AMPI 1, AMPI 2, AMPI 3 . . .

Sitting at her school desk, Maribé learned about the life of the continent by reading *African Pages*, selections from authors such as Bernard Dadié, Birago Diop, Camara Laye, Aké Loba, Ousmane Socé . . . She enjoyed the famous schoolbook *Mamadou and Bineta*, and she adored the adventures of Leuk the Hare and of Moni Mambou. She could recite by heart the story of Toto and Nama, two innocent young children who tugged at the ends of a rope, not knowing that in the end it would snap; the story of Moussikassika the little chick, symbol of the intelligence and savvy of the weakest creatures; that of Samba, victor against the odious Guinnârou, an evil water creature that ate anyone who came near the shore; that of Môr Lâm's Bone, an example of the vice of gluttony, because Môr Lâm faked his own death and preferred to be buried alive rather than share his bone with one of his parents; that of Hoi the Bowman, solitary hunter of moons, a story that teaches the origin of the sun; or that of the old woman who walked with a basket on her back on moonlit evenings.

Regularly, at a chalkboard hung by the dining room window, Kimbembé would teach his daughter the secrets of multiplication, the tricks of addition, the ways of division, and the keys to subtraction. In this way Maribé soon went beyond the straw sticks that school students in Batalébé used for counting.

I found Kimbembé's methods drastic. He lost his temper whenever Maribé failed to respond promptly. He would forget he was dealing with a little child only a few years old. Yet his pedagogy proved effective: Maribé was one of the top students in her school, to the point that malicious gossip claimed her father was always interceding with the principal so the teachers would go easy on his daughter and up her grades.

Frustration

I felt somewhat neglected, relegated to the background, next to these two beings who understood each other so perfectly. Kimbembé would show Maribé around the district. On Sundays he took her into the center of Batalébé, among the men playing checkers and dominoes. In the evening she would be exhausted, her clothes dirty.

When it came down to it, my big frustration was that our daughter didn't look like me, despite what Mam'Soko had suggested when we first arrived in Louboulou. The old woman had only seen her through her dull eyes. Those eyes were no longer able to associate images, compare them, then place them back in their reality.

As for me, I say Maribé is the spitting image of her father, Kimbembé. The same face, the same mannerisms. It bothers her when I watch her; she knows I'm comparing her to Kimbembé. She looks down, hunches over, sometimes moves away from me.

V

Oweto, My Home Village

When I go back several years, I see Kimbembé freshly appointed to Oweto, my home village, the place where my life as a woman began.

Oweto is known throughout the country. It's the birthplace of one of our former presidents, who we called "the Immortal" because the official version taught us that all heroes of the people were immortals. And since the Immortal of Oweto was a hero, we had always believed he was living somewhere alongside other immortals like Che Guevara, Amilcar Cabral, Ben Barka, or Lumumba.

A Disrupted School Year

At the time, news of the arrival in our district of teachers from the South went the rounds of the place. It was the first time that people from other regions were coming to teach in Oweto. The Immortal's government had had to be hard-nosed so as to finally see young instructors from the South agreeing to begin their career in the North, and not even in the big towns like Owando or Impfondo, but in remote spots like Oweto.

Kimbembé arrived in Oweto the year that I failed my middle school leaving certificate. For three months our school had needed new teachers in history, geography, physical education, biology, and French. The principal was infuriated since he had to leave his office, return to the classroom, and teach some of these subjects so as not to leave us behind in relation to other students around the country. But he did it against his will, and it showed. With his thick voice and haughty, even scornful expression, he did not refrain from criticizing the political authorities for the shortage of teachers. For him, a principal ought not to be teaching anymore. During the lessons, his explanations were cursory, vague, and his teaching lacked spirit. He claimed he was just giving us the basics, which we would build on once the specialist teachers came.

We had little idea those teachers would be from the South.

A Frail Young Man

Kimbembé was a frail young man with light skin, of average height, fine features, and a timid demeanor. He arrived one evening on one of the trucks that ran between Oweto and Mapapouville once a quarter. He must have seen the impenetrable night of the region, the massive outlines of the trees that loomed in the darkness like implacable sentinels watching over the shadows. He would have felt the night wind and heard the call of the grass owls in the foliage. He would have noticed the few lamps lit around the main square.

This was Oweto, my birthplace.

The uncanny, unsettling night must have crushed the southerner's ambitions. He may well have imagined that the Ministry of Education had really landed him in it with this appointment. On the other hand, he had the consolation of being posted with other colleagues from the South, and one from the center of the country, whose name was Ngampika. At least he wasn't going to be living alone in this penal colony. Ngampika was our new physical education teacher. The newcomers lived in official housing near the Mboualé River, which had been named for the adoptive mother of our young president, the Immortal. The day they arrived, the housekeepers went to meet them. The principal did not go.

The following day we got a close look at our new teachers as they crossed the main courtyard on their way to the principal's office. The latter received them with a look of sympathy, as if they'd just cut off all contact with civilization. He sighed and gave one of his meanest smiles, of a kind that he alone had mastered. The principal summoned his deputy, for he wasn't going to waste his time on explanations—he who had always thought there wasn't anything worth seeing in our institution. We in the school were thoroughly familiar with his complaints. There was always something lacking. And it was the authorities' fault. If we were allocated new bench desks, he'd grumble that there was a shortage of chalk and inkwells. New supplies would arrive a few days later, but by then the principal was already griping that the flag in the middle of the courtyard was tattered and that it showed a lack of respect to the country to raise the national colors on such a ragged piece of fabric. The authorities had another one delivered, but now the principal muttered that there were more important things than flags—for example, the conditions in which the school administration lived.

Such was our principal . . .

A Guided Tour of the School

On that day the group of new teachers filed after the deputy principal on their tour of the school, listening attentively to his explanations. They viewed the extensive plantations maintained by the students in accordance with the policy of the time, whose slogan was: "One school, one field."

The newcomers also visited the sports field, the little chemistry lab, the cafeteria, and finally the classrooms. After that the group huddled in the teachers' room and remained there for hours while we observed them from a distance, guessing which ones were kind and which were tough . . .

Kimbembé's First Lesson

I'll never forget Kimbembé's first lesson, on the demography of our country. I was fascinated by the knowledge he displayed about our different ethnic groups and languages, and the different human types within the population. We learned that the Téké could be distinguished from the groups of the actual plateaus, from those of the West (the Laali, the Tsangui, the Nzabi) and those of the North (the Koukouya, the Bangangoulou, the Tégué-Alima).

He was precise in his explanations. His way of conveying what he knew contrasted sharply with the gesticulations of the principal. He was markedly younger than the other teachers, most of whom were over fifty. Even Ngampika appeared to be older than him. We figured Kimbembé must be some kind of prodigy. And we waited impatiently for his next lesson. He taught French and history with equal ease. Much later, when he came to help me fill in the gaps in my learning, I would be amazed to hear him explain physics and chemistry, the two subjects that had tripped me up on my school leaving certificate.

Obsession

As the weeks passed, I imagined more and more that he was watching me as he taught. Was it my imagination? His gaze would single me out; he seemed to be addressing me privately.

When our eyes met, I would look down. He sometimes gazed at me for a moment with a faint smile that bothered me.

Deep down I was beginning to get used to seeing him. He had a presence, a belief in what he was saying. The admiration I'd come to have for him paralyzed me. I recorded my feelings in little pink notebooks. I wrote that I was in love with this southerner who would never be able to look at me from close up. I assigned all kinds of qualities to him. I wrote poems to him, in the style of the "recitations" of French poets that were part of our program. I imitated the poems of Ronsard or Lamartine, putting a man in place of the woman glorified by those famous poets. I no longer felt at ease during his classes. I was convinced he read the poems in my pink notebooks.

The Man from the Center

Ngampika, our physical education teacher, cultivated an air of mystery about his origins. It amused me to see him laying claim to one camp one day, the next day another. What was certain was that he was born in the central region of our country. Now, southerners think that people from the center are northerners, whereas the northerners count the center as part of the South. So Ngampika could say he was from either region, depending on what suited him at the moment.

Kimbembé's Advocate

When my girlfriends criticized Kimbembé during the break, I would leap to his defense. The criticisms concerned his southern origins. In contrast to Ngampika, he made no secret of the fact that he was from Batalébé, which was known nationwide as one of the bastions of opposition to all the northern regimes.

Kimbembé's presence upset many older people in Oweto, who muttered in a disgruntled tone: "This place is really going to the dogs! They send us these types from the South as if we northerners weren't smart enough to teach our own children!"

At home, my two younger brothers and I would talk about it. They mostly just made fun of our teacher's Afro. My parents, on the other hand, reacted like the other people in Oweto. I heard my father sigh one evening almost in resignation: "The authorities have shown us that folks from the South are cleverer than us . . ."

VI

Gardening Duty

I had never known any man before Kimbembé. In the district of Oweto, love relations are taken seriously. They have to end in marriage. You can't sully the reputation of a family by having a relationship with no future.

In Oweto, news travels fast. Everyone knows what everyone else is doing. Gossip spreads like a flooding river. That was why I never let Kimbembé kiss me outside, even in the bushes around the village when we were alone.

I realized I truly was in love with him the day I refused to go weed the yard in the teachers' compound. This was a duty for most middle schools and high schools in Vietongo. Every two weeks, two students did yard work where the teachers lived. I regarded this as an imposition, and I'd acquired a reputation as a rebel, which endured despite the punishments imposed upon me by the principal.

It was a Friday afternoon.

We did not have classes. I knew that if I went to the teachers' compound with another girl from my class, I would meet Kimbembé. I wouldn't be able to control myself. I'd be shaking. He'd see.

My classmate arrived on time, but I hadn't even gotten out of bed. I was about to go back to my rebel ways. I was counting on the other girl finishing all the work alone. Afterward I'd go see her, thank her, and we'd agree to keep what had happened a secret. But she wouldn't play along. She made the situation worse by only clearing half the yard.

* * *

First thing Monday I was called to the principal's office. He sat me down and paced up and down around me, his hands behind his back. He shouted, banged on the desk with a wooden ruler, and gestured like an excited monkey. The only excuse I could give was that I'd been unwell. The principal ordered me to finish the other half of the work the following Friday and declared that he personally would come and check up on me.

I'd fallen into my own trap. I'd be alone, without the classmate who could at least have served as a shield if I'd been there the previous Friday. Should I pretend to be ill again? The principal would summon my parents.

The Man and the Book

Toward midmorning I found myself in front of the teachers' compound. There were houses scattered here and there. It was almost a separate little village. I found a hoe in the bamboo hut that served as a storeroom for the school. I was wearing a white T-shirt with a wax wrap dress around my waist. I left my sandals and my bag on a small hillock. The Mboualé flowed a few yards away. I sharpened the hoe on a rock and began working near the waterside.

Now I'd been working for half an hour. I'd overcome the fears I'd had at the beginning. The idea of encountering Kimbembé no longer bothered me. I was sure he wouldn't come out of his place before midafternoon.

I gradually approached the houses. I suppressed the urge to sing, the way I used to when I'd work in the fields with my parents. I was already sweating—the sun was at its highest. The nearby trees guarded the shade at their feet. My eyesight faltered.

When I raised my head, in front of me I saw an open window a few yards away. A man with a book in his hand was watching me work. He might have been there a while.

Kimbembé could not have been more discreet.

The hoe fell from my hand. My whole body felt awkward. Our teacher greeted me with a wave of his left hand. He stayed where he was, right in the middle of the window, his hand still raised.

Uneasy, I went on nervously clearing the yard. The hoe kept getting stuck in the ground, and I had to strain to prize it loose. I even worked over areas where there were no weeds. My forehead became more and more covered in perspiration. I had only one thought in my mind: to finish as quickly as possible and run away. The teacher's voice made me jump.

"When you're done working, Mademoiselle Iloki, don't forget to come say good-bye to me."

The Omelet

When the job was finished around twelve thirty, I jumped for joy: the teacher was no longer standing in the window. What a stroke of luck.

I planned to make my escape along the river. I took the rake and the hoe and headed back to the hillock to pick up my things. At that moment Kimbembé reappeared. From a distance he was holding out a bottle of cold water to me. I couldn't get away now. I walked around the houses, put the tools in the shed, and spent a few minutes cleaning up in the river.

I knocked hesitantly at his door. He asked me in. The pots and pans were hanging on the walls. The bedroom was screened off with a raffia curtain. Kimbembé had set two places at the table. Suddenly becoming aware that I had been standing timidly for several minutes, he asked me to sit down. I explained that I had to be getting back, that my parents were expecting me.

"I've made a nice omelet. Work makes you hungry. Do me the pleasure of sharing the only dish that I know how to make."

I sat to his left.

"No, Mademoiselle Iloki, sit facing me."

I couldn't hold his gaze. He did his best to put me at ease. He told jokes. I laughed, often without understanding, and above all with no decrease in the tension that was oppressing me more and more.

"Mademoiselle Iloki, I saw that you failed your middle school certificate."

"I'm not very good at chemistry and physics," I said in a faint voice.

"Yet those subjects only require a resolute application of scientific reasoning! An exam needs to be prepared for as you go along. Revising in the last few days is not a good idea. You ought to know that learning is opposed to haste. A well-looked-after brain is one that receives information in an orderly fashion. In that way it has time to break it down, chew it over, swallow it, and digest it. When all's said and done, all students are alike: they put their gray matter through a harsh ordeal a few days before the exam!"

I didn't dare draw my plate toward me.

"Please, help yourself, mademoiselle. How old are you?"

"Sixteen and a half," I murmured, my eyes on my dish.

He knew my age. He just wanted to hear me say it out loud. Counting on his fingers, he said: "So you're several years behind in your schooling?"

"I started school a bit late."

"That puts my mind at ease."

The Classics

We were together for an hour.

I finally relaxed. He spoke only about me, about what was best for me. He offered lots of advice about my rebellious behavior. The principal had been complaining. Kimbembé asked me to promise I'd change. I was already thinking about how I could escape. In a shaky voice I indicated that I was leaving.

He vanished into his bedroom and came back with three books.

"I'd like to give you these, they might be of use to you in your compositions."

I got up, barely able to keep upright, and offered him my hand. As he took it, he looked right into my eyes.

"You're a very beautiful northerner."

I smiled, unsettled by this unexpected compliment.

It's always hard to describe oneself objectively, but I must admit that men were not indifferent to me. In Oweto, whenever one of them passed me in the street, he couldn't take his eyes off my chest, first of all, which was that of a grown woman, and my backside, which, so it seemed, moved in a suggestive manner, even though I made no effort at all in this direction. True, I had a way of knotting my wrap dress very tight around my hips, giving a particular curve to my bottom. The men said I was nothing but a little tease.

I took my hand from his.

I was outside. He followed me with his eyes all the way out of the compound.

I turned around and saw him wave his right hand. I waved back.

I went along the riverbank, heading back toward the center of town. Out of curiosity I read the titles of the books he'd given me: *Poetic Meditations* by Alphonse de Lamartine, *The Little Prince* by Antoine de Saint-Exupéry, and *The Plague* by Albert Camus . . .

VII

Family Portrait

My father had not advanced far in his schooling. Just two years of primary school, like many men and women of the generation before Independence. Yet most of the time he made us speak French at home. And each time we would make fun of my mother: she herself had not gone to school at all, but she played along with my father in speaking a garbled approximation to French.

Roger Iloki has a stern face and short gray hair with a parting in the middle. He smiles little and talks a lot. Not especially tall, always dressed in a traditional abacost suit, he prides himself on having raised his three children by virtue of his occupation and on owning a huge house built of durable materials. He was born in Oweto, the home village of his late parents. He thought that the world stopped here, that other parts of the country were degenerate, especially Mapapouville and Pointe-Rouge. He was close to Monsieur Bayo, the local chief, who we called "Chief Bayo." My father was a member of the District Council, along with other Oweto notables. He gave us a strict upbringing. My brothers and I were punished severely whenever we bickered. He wasn't interested in the reason for our arguments. He demanded silence the whole time.

I'm the eldest in the family. My two brothers still live in the North. Neither they nor my parents ever left the region, not even to come visit us in Batalébé. Since the events I've had no word from them. The inhabitants of Oweto do not know telephones or electricity.

Paul runs a small grocery shop in the district. Placide, the youngest, helps Father, who is a respected local mason. The plan is for Placide to take over the business from Father, who taught him the science of the trowel and the set square.

Mother sells smoked fish from a bowl that she carries on her head. She does the rounds of every house in the morning and in the evening. She's a plump woman with very dark skin. Her grandparents were originally from Central African Republic. She doesn't speak Sango, the national language of that country, because she was born in Oweto.

* * *

My father would never have agreed to a southerner, even one with the coveted status of teacher, courting his daughter. In fact teachers are respected in this country. At the start of each school year they're given sheep, roosters, vegetables.

Kimbembé was a skilled strategist who was able to win over my father through my mother, to the point of making him forget his apprehensions and his prejudices concerning the South. Every evening, when my mother would come to the teachers' compound to sell her wares, Kimbembé would spend a long time talking to her. He would pay for fish that my mother wanted to give him for free. He even gave her books to bring home for me. My mother was the first to change her opinion of the man from the South.

One day as we were eating, Lizabeth (we called her by her first name) said in her amusing French: "That Kimbembé, it unbelievable! You think he not even southern man. He is like us, very, very nice. He always buy from me lots, lots fish and give so big book for Hortense."

Private Lessons

Kimbembé was no longer the monster that my parents found so objectionable when he first arrived in the district. People had gotten to know him better, along with his colleague Ngampika, who was from neither the North nor the South and could choose his camp according to what suited him. Aside from our furtive meetings in the bushes, I would visit Kimbembé at his place, as discreetly as possible, whenever he asked me to. The house closest to his was Ngampika's, but the latter's front door and windows were on the other side. Ngampika didn't suspect a thing. I could go to Kimbembé's without his colleagues knowing. In class I hid our relationship, which was taking shape day by day. I concealed it so well that my classmates thought my behavior strange. They found me calmer, more at ease.

To begin with, Kimbembé and I worked on my deficiencies. He even taught me physics and chemistry! He would open the textbooks, read them to me, and explain. But with time his way of looking changed. It stopped being that of a teacher looking at a student and became that of someone who has intimate feelings for another person. He revealed his sentiments one day when he slipped a note in my history book. He wanted me to come to his place after school . . .

Stolen Kisses

I arrived at his house around five in the afternoon. He talked to me about past participles and their agreement. Two places were set at the table. We were going to eat.

After thirty minutes of a private lesson, we took our seats at the table. I sat opposite him without his having to ask me to, like he did the first time I'd set foot in his house. We ate *saka-saka-moukalou*, a local dish made with cassava leaves and smoked fish. Afterward he made tea. He was nervous; his movements became clumsy. I'd never seen him so much on edge.

He walked around the table, abruptly stood behind me, and placed his hands on my shoulders. I wanted to run away, to shout. It was as if I were hypnotized. I could hear his breathing. I turned around and our eyes met.

Encouraged no doubt by my lack of protest, he knelt down in front of me. It was the first time I was going to be kissed by a man. I was ashamed of the desire I was discovering inside myself, which was rendering me passive and voiceless. My senses were alert and I had trouble swallowing my saliva. I didn't notice at which moment my dress fell around my feet. I closed my eyes as his hands began to follow the contours of my burning body, opening me to the life of a woman. I sank into his arms, somewhat complicitous in this game that I was beginning to enjoy.

VIII

The Age of Jesus When He Died

I was seventeen and a half when Kimbembé asked for my hand, just after I passed my middle school leaving certificate. I can say I owed my success in the exam to him. It was thanks to him, to the care with which he'd attended to my education, that I'd managed to achieve one of the highest grades in my cohort. These arguments, though, were not enough to convince my father. Roger Iloki was opposed in principle to the idea of the marriage. He wasn't going to hand his daughter over to a southerner. It was a disaster. Lizabeth was Kimbembé's advocate in our home. She kept stressing how kind Kimbembé was. She pointed out that many northerners were bad people, selfish and lacking a conscience. The two of them would be lucky to have such a cultured and incomparably good-natured son-in-law. She was glad Kimbembé had had the courage to put the question at a time when rumors of our relationship had begun to circulate.

Lizabeth kept up the attack day after day; my father sometimes had to leave the house to get some relief. What bothered Roger Iloki the most was when Lizabeth cornered him, pressed his back to the wall.

"You will be shame if there no marriage, right here, here in Oweto! You daughter will have sleep with South man for nothing for free. Better marriage with South man than South man sleep with your daughter for nothing for free. You think about it good one all day one all night and tell us wha you think!"

Lizabeth's language no longer made anyone laugh—her way of thinking was undeniably to the point. My brothers agreed with her. But even then Roger Iloki wouldn't budge.

"I don't actually know this man. And anyway, why is this happening only to me? I'm sure he's already made love with Tensia, I see her moving her backside in a strange way."

My mother, who had gone to the teachers' compound to sell her fish, had a long discussion with Kimbembé. She assured him that the marriage would take place and that she knew her husband well. Out of pride, Roger refused to change his mind, but when he would leave the house and go get a drink in the neighborhood, that would mean he'd agreed. They'd wait till I turned eighteen.

Kimbembé's mind was put at rest. He was going to ask for a transfer. After you'd worked for two years elsewhere, you had the right to ask to return to your own region. We would go live in the South, in Batalébé. We'd spend a few days in Mapapou-ville on the way.

Roger Iloki and Kimbembé became friends, even though the former found it hard to suppress his prejudices regarding southerners. The two of them could be seen going for a drink together. One day my father asked how old his future son-in-law was. Kimbembé said he'd just reached the age Jesus was when he died.

"So Jesus had an age?"

"Certainly."

"All right, don't tell me, I'll find it out myself."

"I can give you a Bible, Monsieur Iloki."

"No, no, it's fine, my daughter must have one. She and her brothers used to take those kind of classes from some nuns who passed through here."

Roger Iloki, who religiously speaking was more of an animist, was embarrassed to reveal his ignorance about Christianity in front of Kimbembé.

That evening, when I came back from school, my father was waiting for me. He asked me the question point-blank.

"Listen, Tensia, you used to go to that church run by the Whites—how old was Jesus when he died?"

"Thirty-three. Why?"

"There!" he said triumphantly.

"There what?"

"That's the age of your future husband."

IX

A Marriage of National Unity

The notables of Oweto. The principal of my school, who let us use the big hall. Kimbembé's colleagues. My father, wearing his traditional coat, which smelled of mothballs, its creases showing it had been taken out of storage half an hour before. My brothers, dressed in black as if they were attending a funeral. My mother, talkative that day, wearing *misso ya pitin* Dutch wax print wraps. The *biyaoula* on her head amused the crowd, as she'd piled this traditional head covering higher than it should go. Monsieur Bayo's speech was a vibrant hymn to national unity. This was an exemplary marriage. He called on the other inhabitants to follow suit, in an address which I can reproduce here word for word, having recited it to myself for a long time in the months following our marriage:

> We are all Vietongolese. We have the same ancestors, the Bantus. We share the same history. Our beloved president will be happy to learn that a marriage of the farthest points has just taken place!
>
> This land of Oweto will become Kimbembé's land too. He will be able to come settle here whenever he wishes. It is true that the couple have decided to live in the South. That will be an enriching experience for Hortense. Down there she will continue to study so she can complete her high school education.

In the name of our ancestors and of the authorities who govern us, I am delighted by this union, and I wish the newlyweds happiness that will be crowned with descendants, something we all hope for, and which will symbolize the true face of the children of tomorrow: the children of national unity!

May the festivities begin!

The school principal repeated the same ideas in his doughy voice. He strove to vie with the previous speaker in eloquence. He imitated the enthusiasm of the chief of Oweto. He ended by praising Kimbembé in terms that I also used to recite:

He is an exemplary teacher. He is not a teacher who dominates. He persuades, converses, understands, and brings students face to face with their own responsibilities. Kimbembé has grasped the fact that to educate someone means to show them their responsibilities. His professional conscience is beyond question. His future is as dazzling as sunlight bursting through a cloud long rendered dismal by the threat of an imminent storm.

Everyone clapped.

The principal gave a contented belch. He liked to hear himself talk and sought out uncommon words and nonsensical phrases. My father spoke too. He thanked his son-in-law for the sheep, the white rooster, the shotgun, the three demijohns, a Petromax lantern, a trowel, and a sack of cola nuts, things he had asked for as the bride price. My mother had received a Dutch wax wrap dress, a hoe, earrings, and a large bowl for her smoked-fish business.

A pig that had been roasted behind the hall was carved up. There was palm wine. And red wine from France, which Chief Bayo and the principal were fond of. The latter revealed that he had a wine cellar in his house. It contained presents from

Europeans who had passed through Oweto. The principal and Chief Bayo retired to a corner to better appreciate the wine and to talk about France in peace and quiet. But they spoke so loudly that everyone heard them.

The principal was the first to raise his glass. He sniffed it, exaggeratedly copying the actions of a connoisseur.

"Ah, if only we had some camembert it'd be just like in France. Burgundy! The Loire!" he proclaimed.

"Yes, my dear fellow, a good Coulommiers camembert, the kind that reeks from yards away and whose smell repeats on you two days later!" Chief Bayo replied.

The two men burst out laughing. They embraced, congratulated one another, as if they were sharing recollections of France, whereas in fact neither of them had ever visited that country.

* * *

Everyone agreed it was a fine celebration. It remained in local memory. Chief Bayo had us exchange rings after another poignant speech. My father sat there somberly, like a declawed lion. He was not accustomed to smiling, though he made an effort for the occasion.

A dusty old record player was brought out to loud cheers. We played 33s and 45s. Even when the needle coughed over the grooves, everyone still shouted "encore!" at the end of each song. We danced to the rhythms of the almighty Franco's OK Jazz, to Tabu Ley Rochereau and the Orchestre Afrisa International, as well as to the Three Brothers (Youlou Mabiala, Loko Massengo, and Michel Boyibanda). My parents waited for the classics from the time of Wendo Kolosoy and Grand Kallé before heading out onto the dance floor. They thrilled to the voice of the last mentioned as he sang "Independence Cha Cha."

The Cuban

How could I omit from this notebook the character of Vincent Komotié, a sergeant in the national army, who at that time we called "the Cuban" and who, as if by magic, brought along Cuban music. He was one of the few people in the district who had actually been to Cuba. He'd spent some time there as part of the military exchanges in those days.

When he showed up with his records, the guests thronged him, begging him to share his reminiscences, though there wasn't a soul in Oweto who hadn't already heard them.

Clearing his throat, he made a show of yielding reluctantly to the wishes of the majority. He held his records under his arm, as if he were afraid someone would pinch them. In no time at all he had catapulted us into the city called Santiago de Cuba, which not one of us could have located on a map of the world.

"That place is a wonder!" he said ecstatically, his eyes damp with nostalgia. "May those who have ears, listen! Though it's imagination I need, not just ears, which even donkeys have. Santiago de Cuba! Don't talk to me of that city! I wandered among the populace, along the thoroughfares filled with crowds, music, noise. At times I'd take an old taxi whose black exhaust fumes even clouded up the front of the vehicle! But that was the atmosphere, that was the life. I'd occasionally eat at one of the local places, in a convivial setting, and I'd be served Havana Club Añejo Reserva rum, on the house. I wasn't interested in drinking piña coladas like a common tourist—no! What do you imagine?

"The little chicas, each one prettier than the last, they all chased after me: very dark Negro women, girls with skin like terra-cotta, others with smooth and gleaming black hair, those whose skin was like a Seville orange, others with eyes like fountains dazzling in the sunlight. And that's not even the half

of it! You get the picture? I'd take a seat on the terrace of the
Hotel Casa Granda, enjoying the delights of a Cohiba cigar or a
Romeo y Julieta or Montecristo, while in the background there
was music by Compay Segundo, Eliades Ochoa, Ibrahim Fer-
rer, Los Van Van, 'Hasta Siempre,' Carlos Puebla, or Guillermo
Portabales with his big hit 'El Carretero,' which we'll hear in
just a minute. And then, which of you can resist the piano of
Don Rubén González?

"From my place on the terrace of the Casa Granda, I could
keep an eye on the Plaza de la Revolución. All I had to do was
snap my fingers for one of the mixed-blood chicas to come sit by
me and lay her head on my shoulder. I was the pope of Santiago
de Cuba. I'd march through the city with a delegation of Cuban
men and women, buying them Cerveza Cristal left, right, and
center. I couldn't have cared less if the earth was round or flat,
whether it turned around itself and the sun or didn't move at
all. I was alive, I was breathing! We'd walk about the city, my
friends and me: Billy the Kid from Benin, Yapi the Millionaire
from Côte d'Ivoire, Alassane the guy with the Vespa, who traf-
ficked cigars, and Alino, a.k.a. Monsieur Fubu.

"In the evening, let me tell you, the nights were thrilling. I'd
spray myself liberally with eau de cologne, because those girls
loved eau de cologne! There were all kinds of classy places I
could choose from: the Tropicana, La Casa de la Música, La
Claqueta, and above all Club 300, where I learned the three
steps of true salsa, Cuban salsa: the *dilequeno*, or half circle
behind your partner, with a quick thrust on the left foot,
coordinated with the lady; the *sombrero*, with your arms crossing, like two praying mantises making love. And all this amid
indescribable elegance! I was no longer Vincent but Vicente!"

The Cuban of Oweto demonstrated his technique, but no
woman in the district could keep up with him in what we

termed his convoluted moves. The women of Oweto preferred the Vietongolese rumba.

* * *

In the meantime, across the room, annoyed by the Oweto Cuban's vanity, Chief Bayo and the principal were tipsily singing songs by Yves Montand, Charles Trenet, and Bourvil. The Cuban disappeared, and I never saw him again before we left the district.

Kimbembé held me very tightly, as if I might get away from him at any second. This was the moment to talk to him about something that had been preoccupying me for several days, though I was apprehensive about his reaction.

I led him aside.

"Don't hold me so hard like that!"

"Why not? You're not embarrassed to be close to me in front of your family, are you?"

"No, you're in danger of crushing the head of your unborn child. I've not had my period for forty-three days."

X

The Transfer

Three months after our marriage, with the support of the principal and Chief Bayo, Kimbembé got his transfer to the South in time for the new school year, with a promotion as a bonus. He would be teaching at the high school instead of the middle school. This posting had been easy to arrange, the more so because the principal had insisted I should continue my education at high school, a level that did not exist in Oweto or the surrounding area.

For his part, Chief Bayo wrote to his superiors. He pointed out that the transfer would be a kind of national understanding: the husband having come to know the North, it was now desirable that the wife should discover the South.

* * *

We weren't able to take all our things. Some remained behind with my parents.

I was experiencing fatigue. I'd passed the first trimester. It still wasn't visible. I told Kimbembé he should leave his trunk of books in the North. Really I was just joking.

"Out of the question! That trunk is a gold mine, Hortense. I inherited it from my grandfather. It's older than you, and you owe it respect. It's thanks to the trunk that today you've been able to read the great French authors. I breathe with it, walk with it; I live with Proust, Balzac, Stendhal, Gide, and the others!"

An Uneasy Father

It was the first time I was going to leave Oweto. My brothers were devastated. They hadn't understood that the marriage would impose a distance between the couple and each spouse's family. For them I was a kind of second mother. There was a special bond between us.

They wouldn't hear my voice anymore. They wouldn't see me coming and going in the house. Now they began to resent this man who was taking away a part of their existence. If they'd realized it before, they would have sided with our father in opposing the marriage. The majority would have carried the day. They'd taken my mother's side because I loved Kimbembé.

I tried to console them by telling them that I'd be thinking of them. That I'd come back to visit. That marriage wasn't death; it was a happiness. That they too would get married in their turn and would leave our home.

My parents spent the night lavishing advice on me. We were setting off the next day.

"You never know with southerners," my father said as if he were delivering a funeral oration. "I didn't say no to this marriage, I didn't say yes, but your mother convinced me, she and your brothers. Fine. But now you're leaving us, and we've no idea where the South is, and this little Batalébé place. That's not right! What's certain is that it's very, very far away and that it's easier to go to Central African Republic even, than to the village where you'll be living. All the same, this man is a decent person, because he's transformed you. He's made you one of the most outstanding students in the Oweto school. You were congratulated on your certificate by the high-ups, who keep a close eye on things. The principal told me. Kimbembé's a good man, like us northerners. But will he be able to stay that way among those who aren't? For our part we've known the man by day, but you're the only one who'll get to see him by night, in his own region. Come back to Oweto as often as you can, because we care about our grandchild who's going to be born."

XI

The Longest Journey

We made the journey by truck.

It took us more than three days to even get to Mapapouville. From there we were going to take another truck to Batalébé.

On the way Kimbembé dozed, his head resting on his trunk of books. Mapapouville was a very long way from the North. We slept in villages about which I have no recollection.

The truck would stop. They'd stretch out tarpaulins, and the travelers would jostle for the little space available. The next day we'd continue on our way.

When we reached Mapapouville we were exhausted. We were supposed to leave again two days later, but Kimbembé decided we'd take a break and stay for another seven or eight days. He wanted to show me the political capital, which I was seeing for the first time.

Discovering Mapapouville

We took a room at the Le Rail Hotel near the Central Station of the Vietongo-Ocean Railroad. Later on, the Le Rail would become a kind of second home for us. We'd spend the dry season there almost every year, during the school vacation.

Mapapouville had grown up along the right bank of the Vietongo River. It covered about twenty-one square miles and had a population of over nine hundred thousand. It was quite a change from the little district of Oweto that we'd come from.

Kimbembé knew the city. It was where he'd completed his higher education and taken his school-teaching exam. As a college student he'd had a little room at 1409 Avenue Loutassi on the Plateau des 15 Ans.

He wanted to go see his old neighborhood and the house he'd lived in. We went there one afternoon. We took a bus from behind the hotel, not far from the prime minister's residence. It crossed the bustling neighborhoods of Poto-Poto and Moungali and dropped us at the start of the Avenue Loutassi.

Cars honked their horns back and forth at each other. Children played in the streets. Kiosks selling cigarettes and Kojak lollipops lined the main roads. The café-bars vied with one another in music, their tables and stools out in the public space. Passersby would stop, listen to the music curiously, then, unable to help themselves, perform dance moves to the general acclamation of the public and the vehicles threading their way through the crowd. Kimbembé had experienced similar scenes during his student days.

He showed me the Eden Café, across the street from the house where he'd lived as a student.

"This is one of the busiest cafés on the plateau. The Parisians, the Sapeurs, come here every evening to display their cars and their clothes."

"Parisians, Sapeurs?" I said, confused by the city jargon.

"Right. They're young people from this country who live in France. They ended up there out of a sense of adventure. They call themselves *Sapeurs*, from *SAPE*: the Society for Atmosphere and Personal Elegance. They whiten their skin with Nigerian products and buy designer clothes from the grand couturiers of the famous Rue du Faubourg Saint-Honoré, then show them off back here during their vacations. The Eden is considered their locale of choice. It has the advantage of being situated right along the edge of the avenue. That way the dandies, who come from the Bleu-Blanc-Rouge neighborhood, can line up their Solex bikes or their cars with Paris plates. When they arrive in the evening, the *nguémbos* are waiting for them in the entrance to cheer them on as they hand out a few French francs or Parisian metro tickets to those aficionados."

The Student Dormitory

A large, unfinished, grim-looking house with a long hallway, doors on either side, and a small interior courtyard. This was where Kimbembé the student had stayed. Each door had a number. All around there were other uncompleted buildings, right up to where the runway of Mapapouville Airport started. A little farther down the avenue you could see a series of permanently constructed residences, houses in marble, copies of European châteaux. The politicians and civil servants lived there.

I was somewhat surprised to learn that the student house belonged to one of the southern politicians, a legendary figure by the name of Kaya-Kaya. According to the official version, he had been implicated in the assassination of the Immortal President. Kaya-Kaya had been killed in that very house by a group of soldiers. As a student, for three years Kimbembé had rented the room next to the one in which the historic leader of the South had met his end. He told me he'd found the place thanks to an acquaintance who was a close friend of the late Kaya-Kaya's older brother. This friend, a man with greedy eyes, would come to collect the rent a day before the end of the month, early in the morning, when the students were still brushing their teeth before heading out to the university.

The Eden and Its Regulars

Before we left the Plateau des 15 Ans, we took a table at the Eden, where we were served well-chilled Kronenbourgs. The late afternoon seemed quiet, yet the regulars began elbowing past one another as they came in. Kimbembé smiled at them, thinking that some of them would recognize him. His attention was drawn by a corpulent, gray-haired man who burst into the place. He hesitated a moment, then chose a seat at the far end, where he could barely be noticed.

"Watch what's going on over there, Hortense, you won't believe me! You see that guy? He reminds me of the good old days. Really, nothing has changed in this city! Generally speaking, at the Eden every spot has its meaning for those in the know. The man who just sat down over there is waiting for one of his latest conquests."

"How can you tell?" I asked, turning blithely around to look at the new arrival. "No, that man could be our father," I added.

"I can even tell you that the conquest is certainly a married woman. When we used to live here, people from high society, betrayed husbands, would give us a banknote to let them know when their wife was in the café. As soon as we thought we recognized them based on the brief description they'd given, we'd jump in a taxi or call the man we'd later refer to as our 'benefactor.' We made a little pocket money that way."

Kimbembé didn't have time to finish his story: a tall woman with an imposing backside, wearing a Dutch wax outfit, got out of a cab. She looked around as if to make sure no one was following her; then she stole hurriedly into the café and headed for the corner where the corpulent man was already in raptures at her arrival. The lovers kissed on the mouth. The woman sat down with her back to us, and they started talking in hushed tones. Beforehand the man had spoken a few words to the waiter and discreetly slipped him a banknote. The server had nodded with a complicitous smile and had indicated an inconspicuous staircase that led to the second floor of the establishment. The man went ahead of the woman, and the couple, in accordance with Kimbembé's conjecture, entered one of the short-term rooms of the Eden. The two lovers only came out an hour later, just as we were getting ready to leave. The woman's hair was mussed up at the sides, and the man's shirt collar was inside out.

Boules D'ambiance

Kimbembé walked me all over the capital. We visited monuments, official buildings—especially the presidential residence, which we could only see from a distance. The cab driver, who'd been chatty when we set off, abruptly fell silent as we drew near to it.

"Don't look in that direction," he said, "or they'll write down my plates. I have children to feed."

So we drove by, looking the other way. We also saw the markets in Bacongo, Talangaï, Poto-Poto, and Ouenzé, and the sellers along the Vietongo River, at the Beach, from where you can see the country closest to our own, the Republic of Nzadi.

In the evenings, a few steps away from the Le Rail, an old Beninese woman with scarifications on her face sold corn mash and *boules d'ambiance* fritters. We'd sit down in the middle of the crowd. The conversations would be about everything: politics, the president's mistress, the people who lived across the river and who were taking jobs away from the Vietongolese, or the most recent crimes that were terrorizing the Mapapouvillians. We would go from laughter to tears. The old Beninese woman would fan her fire with a large aluminum can lid. Blinding smoke would billow from the firepit and almost choke her clients, though they didn't seem to mind. Other such small businesses abounded in the city. We went back several times to that place. I liked the corn mash, which only Beninese women knew how to make. Their Vietongolese rivals, driven by jealousy, claimed that these "foreigners," who were also known as *popos*, prepared their dish with a liquid made back in their home country by grand masters of voodoo. According to the Vietongolese women, that was why customers flocked to the stalls of the *popos* till two or three in the morning.

For me Mapapouville was a marvel. I felt the same emotion every time Kimbembé and I went back. We'd take the train. One time alone we flew, leaving from the airport at Mabombo after a six-hour truck journey. Kimbembé had wanted me to fly in a plane at least once in my life. It was a small-engine machine that seemed to lose its balance every time it entered turbulent air. The engine cut out, then started up again, though the pilots and flight engineers remained calm. The landing was so rough that several passengers were thrown from their seats despite the safety belts. All the same, we arrived safe and sound.

The other times I was the one who insisted on traveling by train. Planes still scare me even today.

XII

The Sacrifice of the Bride

It took us more than nine days to get to Batalébé, in an Isuzu truck crammed with noisy, restless travelers. We fended off pigs, sheep, roosters, whose owners had put them on the vehicle's few wooden seats. We kept stepping in the excrement of these creatures. Kimbembé assured me that this was typical of travel in the backcountry.

I was silent, oppressed by anxiety. My life was changing from one day to the next. Leaving my family. Leaving my native district. Going to live miles and miles away, in a different world. I was aware of the sacrifice that weighed down the shoulders of the wife. The husband had the better role to play. I suddenly felt like a piece of merchandise in the hands of Kimbembé, though I loved him. What difference could I see between me and his trunk of books? Just like the trunk, I was being transported in this truck. We were both subjected to the same jolts. We'd inhabit the same house. The trunk would remain motionless; I could walk and talk. That was the only consolation.

It was hard to get such ideas out of my head. Erasing my past in a single stroke. Going far away from the roofs of home, like a dead leaf separated from its branch. Did Kimbembé notice the tears that I wiped away as quickly as they appeared?

The Moukoukoulou Dam

I told myself we would never get to Batalébé. I kept vomiting, perhaps because of the smell of animal waste and the lack of fresh air inside the truck. I no longer saw the varying landscapes that passed on either side. I slept. I woke up. The journey went on, winding, steep and unpredictable, with perilous bridges and endlessly uneven terrain.

This painful, interminable drive showed the distance between the North and the South of Vietongo, between Oweto and Batalébé. The South of the country looked red, dusty, the grass was high, the sky low and stormy. Villages barely a few miles apart. Unused, impassable roads. The driver managed, though. As we drew near to a village, groups of children would bustle about, clapping and surrounding the vehicle. The driver's assistant would busy himself putting chocks under the wheels. And we'd stop for the night on the main square, encircled by villagers outdoing one another in hospitality.

When we reached the Moukoukoulou Dam, Kimbembé was jubilant.

"Batalébé's close now, we'll be there in less than half an hour!"

At the dam, officials stopped the truck and conducted a routine inspection. Our luggage was turned inside out, rifled through, searched with a fine-tooth comb. Could I have imagined that, at that time, among the Moukoukoulou functionaries was an individual named Gaston Okemba, a northerner like me, who was the husband of the woman who would later become my best friend in Batalébé, Christiane Kengué? He must have been there, among the others, freshly appointed to his post, after working for years at the port of Pointe-Rouge.

XIII

A Mixed Couple in Batalébé

The main square. Houses of sheet metal or straw. The central market. The hospital. We lived in a mud-brick house. It belonged to Kimbembé's parents, who had moved six miles or so away. His father was a potter; he was a man of medium height with an impassive face. He came to see us once a month, accompanied by his wife, Véronique Boutoto, who we called "Mâ Boutoto" out of respect. She kept a close eye on my pregnancy. When she came to visit, she brought bitter-tasting potions that I had to drink in front of her.

"This one will make it so you have a girl, believe me!" she would assure me with absolute composure.

She dreamed of a girl, whereas her husband, Tâ Kimbembé, predicted it would be a boy. They treated me like a daughter. From time to time we'd go out to their village, a quiet spot surrounded by mountains and giant trees. We'd sometimes stay there for a few weeks during the dry season. I would accompany Mâ Boutoto to the fields. We had to walk and walk to reach her plantations of groundnuts, corn, and root vegetables. In the evening I would be exhausted, but we'd have to make dinner. I'd pound the cassava leaves and the palm nuts while she carved a leg of dried wild boar that had been hanging above a sort of little basket by the fireplace.

Life in Batalébé

In that place encircled by creepers, bamboo, and flame trees, life seemed to spread itself out and flow by slowly. The men and women—farmers, hunters, or shopkeepers—wore carefree expressions, I found. They were never in a hurry. The Batalébé area was cut off from the rest of the country. In the morning I would get up very early. I'd sweep the yard and water the plants—I kept a little garden behind the house. Kimbembé would prepare his classes over the weekend; from Monday to Friday he'd leave for work around seven in the morning. He would come back home in the evening, tired out. He'd sit in a woven chair and tell me about his day. I'd listen as I peeled potatoes or cut up vegetables while he helped. My belly grew heavier and heavier.

It was at that time there was a conflict between Kimbembé and the midwife at the Batalébé hospital. He was insisting on being present in the room the day I had the baby. The affair was talked about all over the district. I was no longer able to avoid the gaze of the local people.

Despite all this, I can say I had good conditions for the delivery. I gave birth to a girl, much to Tâ Kimbembé's regret but Mâ Boutoto's satisfaction. A few months afterward I was going to have to begin high school. As I waited, I spent my days at home. I was a little bored when Kimbembé wasn't there. I needed to get out of the house, explore the district, see other people's lives. Yet I felt a certain apprehension. I couldn't have said where it came from, since I felt safe sitting at home watching Maribé sleep. I read, knitted, or braided my hair.

Meeting Christiane for the First Time

One day when Kimbembé was at the high school, I decided to take our daughter for a walk toward the market in the center of the district. She was two and a half months old. The previous day I'd braided my own hair, as I usually did. I managed using two mirrors.

I walked along the side of the dusty main road, Maribé strapped on my back with a wrap. Near the first stalls of the market, a woman came up to us with a big smile. She was wearing a white T-shirt that showed her bust to advantage, and a wrap dress that clung to her curves. She stopped in front of us. She was taller than me; she had light skin and drawn-back hair. Her basket was full of vegetables. She put it down. In an unconstrained way, she touched my hair and turned back the edge of the wrap to see Maribé.

"What a beautiful little angel you have, Madame Kimbembé!"

Taken aback that she knew my name, I retreated a step. She went on.

"Your husband is quite a man! To dare to stand up to the entire staff of the hospital and write letters to ministers!"

"He was within his rights, Madame . . . ?"

"My name is Christiane Kengué. My husband is from your region. He works at the Moukoukoulou Dam."

"How did you know I'm from the North?" I asked, once again surprised.

"There are no secrets in Batalébé. There are so few northerners here that those who come are as plain as flies in a pan of milk! My husband, Gaston, had the same impression to begin with. But later you become used to it, things get mixed up, and you even forget your little piece of native soil. Try to learn our languages, don't shun the community, or you'll be accused of who knows what. Gaston and I would be delighted to get to know you. We could arrange that right now, woman to woman."

"I should discuss it with Kimbembé first."

"That's quite understandable, Madame . . . ?"

"Hortense."

"Yes, Hortense."

She touched my hair again. This familiarity made me uncomfortable. But I quickly learned the meaning of her gesture.

"Your braids are lovely, Hortense! Who did them for you?"

"I did them myself."

"You don't say!"

"Really."

"Well then, I think I'm in luck! I'm also in the habit of braiding my own hair, but it always makes my shoulders hurt from turning around, keeping my hands up in the air and my neck turned to one side. This is a real bit of good fortune, Hortense! We could take turns at braiding each other's hair."

Her joyful nature contrasted with my reserve. After all, though, her suggestion touched me. When she spoke, her face lit up with sincerity and a deep kindness, and it was hard not to say yes. Before we parted, she stroked Maribé's hair and kissed her on the cheek, in passing straightening one of my braids that the wind had blown out of place.

"We live on the other side of the center, near the river. You have to follow the main road and cross the Mampembé Cemetery. It's easy to find: it's the only house around there."

The two of us arranged to meet again at the market two days later. Kimbembé was fine with it. Nor did he say no to Gaston and Christiane Okemba's invitation to go eat with them one day.

The First Dinner

It was our first visit to Gaston and Christiane's. We went over on a Sunday afternoon. Gaston Okemba was there, tall, with a well-trimmed mustache. Christiane wore a headscarf and a pink apron. In her right hand she was holding a wooden spoon, which from time to time she plunged in a large aluminum cooking pot placed on a three-stone fireplace. The fire sent smoke up as far as the trees. She said she preferred cooking outdoors. It seems the food has a different taste. Little Maribé was asleep. I'd put her down on the sofa in the living room. I went back out to Christiane, though she tried to stop me.

"You're our guests, you don't have to lift a finger."

I insisted. In the end she agreed. So I helped her put wood on the fire. I set the table, which stood in the shade of a large mango tree in the middle of the yard.

In the meantime our husbands were getting to know one another, sitting a few yards away with a liter of palm wine. They were roaring with laughter. Gaston was calling my husband "professor."

"Listen, my good friend, 'Kimbembé' would be preferable to this pompous title of 'professor,'" the person in question said, not without a certain false modesty.

Gaston described in detail his work at the Moukoukoulou Dam. Kimbembé earned himself an explanation of the terms *rock-fill dam*, *gravity dam*, and *arch dam*. Christiane whispered to me that her husband would never stop. That he'd done the same thing to her. That he'd end by bringing up the legends surrounding the dam. Well, at least he'd stopped talking about his former duties as customs officer in Pointe-Rouge, and hers at the downtown post office.

Afterward, as I expected, their conversation turned to literature. They reviewed French writers. Gaston liked the Romantic poet Lamartine and recited a few verses of his poem "The Lake." Kimbembé found Lamartine a little whiny; he preferred Rimbaud or Baudelaire.

"Rimbaud? A pretentious young upstart! Plus, what the hell was he doing going to Africa instead of just keeping on writing his poems? Eh? Trying to get rich? Since when have poets had anything to do with being rich? A true poet should write, die poor, and maintain the legend! I'm telling you, Rimbaud was lucky the other guy, that buddy of his—what was his name again—right, that's it, that his buddy Verlaine only wounded him with his gun!"

Despite disagreeing with Kimbembé, Gaston was relishing the fact that he was sitting with an interlocutor who shared his passion. He let my husband know it.

"I can't take any credit, my friend. I'm a literature teacher. When it comes down to it, like everyone else I only talk about what I know."

"I've often dreamed of writing," Gaston confided, "but I don't think I'll ever succeed. That's just how it is. I've given up on the idea. One day I'll clear out my things. Burn all those useless bits of paper. There are people who are made for that, and I'm just getting in their way!"

"My friend, from reading the biographies of several authors, especially those I teach, I've come to the conclusion that writing is a dangerous venture. And like any venture, it has its ups and downs. People of the pen write because they're not capable of doing otherwise. They're driven by an invisible demon that follows them everywhere like the eye of Cain. They're stuck with themselves, facing a world that seems increasingly narrow. How does someone become a writer? When? It's a mystery! If you'll allow me, I'm tempted to paraphrase the novelist Céline and say that people write 'when you have so much music in you that you make life dance' . . ."

"Céline? Never heard of him. With a woman's name like that, he's likely to be waiting for centuries before I get around to reading him! He's not one of those new French authors who bore readers with the state of their soul for hundreds and hundreds of pages, is he?"

"Dinner's ready! Come to the table, my dear intellectuals!" exclaimed Christiane.

* * *

That dinner sealed the friendship between our two couples. Yet our husbands, busy with their work, didn't see each other as often as Christiane and I did. Kimbembé lent Gaston his copy of *Journey to the End of the Night*. After six months of laborious reading, Gaston still hadn't gotten through it. He had the impression of endlessly beginning again, he said. Or it may have been that the moment he set it down, the Céline who was haunting him tiptoed into his bedroom, took the book, and added even more paragraphs, making the story more and more complicated and endless. He never finished it. Incidentally, I don't know what happened to that book, which I hope to read one day. I have no idea if Kimbembé ever got it back.

Christiane and I would run into each other every other day at the market. We'd spend a long time discussing, choosing the same foodstuffs, the same jewelry. We continued to see one another, notably that memorable Sunday when she spoke to me of her life and of Pointe-Rouge.

A third person walked along with us, fragile as could be, and we had to keep an eye on her among the market stalls: it was Maribé . . .

The Second Dinner

There was a second meal, at our place this time. Gaston liked my cooking and told me so.

"This chicken in groundnut sauce is delicious!" he said, taking a second helping.

For a long while before we sat down to eat, as on the previous occasion the two men talked of literature. I had to intervene to put an end to their lengthy discussions. In fact, they spent their time looking through the trunk of books. Each title had its history. Kimbembé was thoroughly enjoying himself.

"Ah yes, *The Devil's Pool*. Here, feel this book, smell it! What do you notice? I bought it at the Talangaï Market when I was a student in Mapapouville. It was lying between a cassava stand and a bowl of sweet potatoes. Look on page forty-seven. There's a mark that I wouldn't get rid of for all the tea in China: it's the imprint of the stallholder's right thumb."

"And this one?" Gaston asked.

"*Destinies*? That's another story. You might say it's a great story. I was passing a little kiosk in the Plateau des 15 Ans neighborhood on my way to buy cigarettes. And what do I see? A young man selling groundnuts who's rolling his merchandise up in pages from de Vigny's book! I didn't buy any nuts, but I surprised him when I asked if I could buy the book! That's why that copy is incomplete—it's missing the introduction and a few poems, including 'The Death of the Wolf.' I photocopied everything that was missing at the French Cultural Center.

"I won't even tell you about *Man's Fate*. Poor Malraux, to see himself treated that way! His book was being used to prop up a table in the Le Relax bar—can you imagine that? I had a hard time buying it from them. The owner thought I was some wise guy who didn't have the money for a drink and was trying to pull a fast one on him. Anyway, we need to go eat. Hortense just gave us an ultimatum. We can pick up again after the meal."

* * *

We took turns inviting each other, and ate together twice a month. Sometimes, when she was five or six, Maribé would go spend the night at our friends', even though I felt it would make Christiane sad about not having any children of her own.

XIV

Dr. Rieux

Years passed in that way.

I went to high school till I completed my baccalaureate. Kimbembé decided that I should occupy myself exclusively with Maribé, with her future. University studies would only have separated us, since the university was in Mapapouville.

So I stayed in Batalébé, at home and idle. Visits from my parents-in-law cheered the place up for a few days once in a while. I felt less alone. Mâ Boutoto liked me. I braided her gray hair while Tâ Kimbembé filled his pipe, leaning back against a mango tree. They were fond of their only son. I left them alone to talk with one another in the evening.

After they went home I would return to my solitude. When I didn't go visit Christiane, I would read. I can say without vanity that I read a great deal in the years that preceded the events in Mapapouville. I helped myself to the contents of Kimbembé's trunk. I gobbled up most of the books in it. Of them all, I read Albert Camus's *The Plague* over and again. Three times? Four? Probably more. Of course Kimbembé in his perpetual contrariness reckoned that *The Stranger* was the more accomplished novel, producing arguments to that effect. I didn't give a fig about his opinion. *The Plague* was my favorite book; I consulted it; I marveled at it as a treasure, even if it lacked a cover. It was the same copy that the young teacher had given me in the North.

Even today I can't conceive of another cover for that book. I always think of it as having my own cover, the one I would have liked it to have. The one that's in my dreams. It's a strange image that came out of my reading. I picture a low sky, red as the clay of our cutoff lakes, and walls of disproportionate sizes. Shadows are seated along the bottoms of these walls. Old women. I don't know what it means, but that's how I imagine the outside of that book, whose words seem carved with a scalpel. Whenever I read it, I would admire Dr. Rieux's boldness, his courage, in the face of the calamity that is the plague. I had the feeling of being imprisoned in the city of Oran along with Camus's characters. I still remember the opening scene of the book: poor Dr. Rieux stumbling on a dead rat. What is this creature doing in the middle of the landing? A little detail, and everything begins. The noose tightens more and more, chapter by chapter...

After the Okonongo Affair I never stopped asking myself: Would Vietongo, our country, also experience a plague in its way? If so, I concluded, we lacked a doctor, a good doctor who if possible would be called Bernard Rieux, like in *The Plague*...

PART THREE
THE OKONONGO AFFAIR AND ITS CONSEQUENCES

I

~~~

Already Over a Week in Louboulou

Now that we're far away from Batalébé, we can believe that one day we'll finally make it to Pointe-Rouge. It's the only place that has been spared by the events. Everything the authorities say about Pointe-Rouge amounts to no more than a diversion. I know that now. It's one of the strategies employed to sow confusion and discourage people from heading for the city.

* * *

Life in Louboulou merges with the red dust. Trees losing their leaves. And that shifty river crawling along in its boredom, no longer knowing which way to flow. It mumbles, paws the ground, barely moving the notched water lilies that accompany it all the way into the maze of bamboo and the crisscross of ferns. Who knows under which skies it will finally discharge its melancholy and its sluggishness?

Mam'Soko is here. She passes this way and that. A light, timid figure, she seems to be running after time, a time that is no longer the same as our own and whose patience and stubbornness we would wish to borrow for the journey that awaits us.

We've been here over a week. We took a walk in the late afternoon. We went to pick cassava leaves in one of Mam'Soko's fields. We dug into the soil to find the roots. My thoughts strayed. I wanted to go back, to resume reading my notebooks and writing in them.

When we returned home, I told Maribé to light the three-stone fire and to put the cassava roots in water to boil them. I ground the leaves in a mortar. We still needed palm nuts. The old lady had given us salt and groundnut paste. It was the first time we'd eaten *saka-saka* without palm oil. All the same, Mam'Soko liked it. Night fell. Maribé went to bed. As for me, I wasn't sleepy. I went into the corner where I've been writing the whole time since we arrived. I lit a candle, because there was no more fuel in the hurricane lamp.

I started remembering the Okonongo Affair.

The Okonongo Affair

According to foreign observers, it is unlikely that Pointe-Rouge should be sharing the experiences of Mapapouville, where everything began after the Okonongo Affair.

When I was in Batalébé I heard several versions of the story, including some that were truly unbelievable; I could have filled any number of notebooks in recounting them and cross-checking them so as to separate the wheat from the chaff. So where's the truth in all of it? Which version should be trusted, since a new one pops up every day?

Depending on whether you come from one district or another, your interpretation of the facts can reflect reality or diverge from it. We had always kept our cool, my daughter and I.

* * *

I remember a visit I made to Christiane, just after the Oko-nongo events. Gaston had not yet been interned and was at work. I took the opportunity to have my hair braided, though it was only two weeks since the last time I'd had it done.

On that day Christiane had predicted that the Okonongo Affair would end up spreading to the South of the country. I didn't believe her, perhaps out of ignorance or because I misunderstood what was at stake. I said to her that it was nothing but a quarrel between two men in power, both northerners. How could a conflict between two sister tribes of the North affect the South? Christiane stepped back abruptly, interrupting her braiding. After a moment of silence, she sat down in a woven chair in front of me. In a calm voice, she began:

"Hortense, when you learn who was confronting who in the North, your view of the facts of Okonongo will change."

She narrated the affair to me with such precision that I thought she must have lived through the events herself.

"I agree with you that it concerned two northerners," she went on. "You shouldn't forget that the North of Vietongo is the native region of General Edou. At the time the affair began, he was merely a former president who'd lost the elections and now had come back from a long exile in France. But the general was not a man for defeat. His ambition was to oust his successor, His Excellency Lebou Kabouya. Everyone knew he could do this only by force of arms, since the people had already thanked him for his service five years before! So then, to put the current regime's back up, he undertook a pilgrimage to the North of the country. As you're aware, he was received as a savior, the man that was needed. Old people knelt down before him. He was given gifts. Women wept and threw their arms around him. Men promised their support if only he should ask. He was carried for miles on a raffia armchair, a traditional honor strictly reserved for our customary chiefs.

"Just to be completely clear, Hortense: General Edou in fact wanted to humiliate Ossouki Wapi, the Minister of the Interior, a northerner who had dared to join the government of His Excellency Lebou Kabouya. How could he have offered his services to a president from the South? It was plain to see that on his pilgrimage the general had wanted above all to pass through Okonongo, the native district of this minister labeled a traitor. What better place to humiliate him than his own village, before his ancestors? It was also a way of silencing his tribe. I really don't think you appreciate the impact of the general's visit to that village!"

I didn't say anything.

She looked around, as if she was worried someone might hear us. In a confidential tone she went on.

"So on that day in the North, a sizeable delegation accompanied General Edou toward the backwater that is Okonongo. The general's militia, the famous Romans, invaded the area. The local population had thought they were getting a visit from their only political luminary, the Minister of the Interior. Then they realized it was the general, a man from the neighboring tribe, the stuck-up ones. Opinions were mixed when it came to this unexpected appearance. Some saw it as the general wishing to make peace with his brothers of the North. Others, more clear-sighted, called it a provocation. They were going to be embarrassed for all to see, especially once they saw the general being carried into Okonongo on his armchair, accompanied by a jubilant crowd."

"You'd think the general was in some way expected in that region!" I put in.

"Moving the story along, you could put it like that, since the general's failure in the elections five years earlier had mortified the northerners, who up till then had gotten used to running the entire country themselves. Trust me, in that respect the Okonongo district was simmering as never before! Cries of joy mingled with insults flung at the visitor. The Romans had their work cut out. The mood was more and more strained between the groups that tried to draw near to the general and the Romans pushing them back onto the grass verge along the road. The procession inched its way through the dense, noisy crowd. No one had imagined the district could produce so many men, women, children. What was certain was that people from the neighboring towns had come in."

"But the Voice of the Vietongolese Revolution said that the general was legitimately defending himself and that all he did was respond to an attack by supporters of the minister!"

"Those are lies! Nothing but lies! In fact things didn't happen the way they were explained on the national radio station, which is controlled by the general. The analysis on Radio-Intercontinentale is the most accurate, but to pick up that station during the events you had to have a radio with a dish antenna like the one we have, which Gaston got while he was working as a customs officer in Pointe-Rouge. The reality is that at the moment the general's procession began to leave the Okonongo district, bursts of gunfire were heard. The local people panicked, while the general and a handful of his Romans in his jeep roared away in a cloud of dust. Other Romans, who had stayed behind to oversee the departure of the procession, entered the center of Okonongo, submachine guns in hand. There were certainly clashes between the general's supporters and locals loyal to the minister. But the provocation definitely came from the Romans themselves, who imagined arrogantly that they were already in power. Over a hundred died! Don't believe the figures provided by the Voice of the Vietongolese Revolution, which, as was to be expected, downplayed the number of casualties. The Romans had demonstrated the effectiveness of their weapons and their desire to return to power.

"Like you, many people took the confrontation as an unremarkable settling of accounts between two northern tribes, as you repeated a moment ago. Yet the Okonongo Affair was all of a sudden exported to Mapapouville, and it triggered the events there."

"As for that," I put in, "the Voice of the Vietongolese Revolution reports that the carnage in Okonongo had nothing to do with the conflict in Mapapouville!"

"And how! If you only listen to commentary from Mapapouville, your view will be a caricature of the facts. We know now that after what happened in Okonongo, General Edou barely made it back to Mapapouville with his men, and that the Minister of the Interior quickly went on the radio to announce that his uncle and his mother had perished in the massacre. Those responsible for such a bloodbath could not go unpunished, he had explained to President Lebou Kabouya. Pursuing the culprits, bringing them to justice: those were the official motives that would trigger the hostilities. President Lebou Kabouya soon issued an arrest warrant for a certain number of people whose names had been mentioned by witnesses to the clashes. The witnesses were certain: the aggressors had been officers, General Edou's trusted men—his Praetorian Guard. In a word, the Romans.

"How do you think those in power might have reacted, eh? So then, in broad daylight, watched by a terror-stricken population, a unit of elite marksmen, a tank, and four jeeps filled with soldiers were dispatched toward the northern sector of Mapapouville with the aim of apprehending the alleged culprits of Okonongo, who, it was said, had taken refuge in the general's residence! The latter learned about the expedition well in advance, thanks to his network of informers. These had provided details of the plans for the operation and when the government militiamen, the Anacondas, would arrive. Which meant that the Romans were already lying in ambush at strategic points in the neighborhood and that the Anacondas were venturing into the lion's jaws. Everyone knows the general's mansion: a huge building towering over other houses in the vicinity. It's a veritable marble château, with a swimming pool, a gigantic fountain, and well-tended grounds. From there the general can oversee a good part of the city. As it happens, by night he likes to gaze at the string of lights that begins at the Centenaire Bridge, zigzags toward the shanty town of Loumfui, then disappears behind the Central Mapapouville Cemetery. There are rumors, which I believe, that underneath his house he built a soccer field, a tennis court, and a screening room. In a word, an entire neighborhood unto itself.

"But wait till you hear what's next, Hortense: the Mapapouville that you knew would become a battlefield after the Okonongo Affair. The rumble of tanks and armored cars, the sound of gunfire, the explosions of grenades transformed the capital into a city experiencing an endless eclipse. The inhabitants felt as if night had fallen. Men from the two factions moved about, heads down, guns trained ahead so as to unsettle the adversary. Then gunfire would ring out right at that moment. The Romans, well disciplined, protected by bulletproof vests, emerged left, right, and center, dropped from the trees and descended from rooftops, pincering the Anacondas, who had no recourse but to fall back. Yet behind them more Romans opened fire and tossed grenades. The local residents barricaded themselves in their houses, their windows shattering from the explosions. Shots went back and forth without respite.

"Little by little, things quietened down in front of General Edou's residence. This was an encouraging sign for the putschists. It meant that the Anacondas had bolted, or were all dead. The Romans outdid one another shooting in the air, their way of celebrating the victory they'd just won."

"But the general and President Lebou Kabouya could just have discussed things and avoided aggravating the situation!"

"That was impossible. They're two strong personalities whose rivalry reaches back into the depths of time. Their respective ancestors were already tearing each other apart over matters of land and chiefdoms. Plus, what do you think would happen to the general's pride? To His Excellence Lebou Kabouya's pretentions to being the first intellectual leader of the country?

"From then on, Mapapouville was divided in two. In the north part of the city, the general and his Romans waited for attacks by those in power but also made serious plans to lay siege to the capital. In the south, His Excellency and the Anacondas dreamed up all kinds of stratagems with a view to disarming their adversary, capturing the wrongdoers, and putting the general on trial for his involvement in the killings. The government increased tenfold the number of soldiers and southern militiamen around the presidential palace, in front of official buildings, and at the homes of leading politicians. The regular army was no longer capable of entering the northern neighborhoods, which had become a proper no man's land protected on all sides by the Romans. Young people were recruited by both camps. Once enlisted and thoroughly brainwashed, they were assigned to the private militias and pledged themselves in the name of God and country. They swore an oath never to retreat in the face of the enemy, and to join the front lines in the fight to conquer the other half of Mapapouville."

"Where was Vercingetorix in all this?"

Christiane paused, her expression blank, as if to gather her thoughts.

"He didn't enter the dance till much later. At the beginning he played the neutrality card, even if he was His Excellency's prime minister. Later, as the situation worsened, he ordered his Negro Grandsons to join forces with the Anacondas. After all, this was an alliance of southerners! What do you imagine? In the two camps, each of them maintained his own preserve. Intimidation campaigns multiplied in the night, with explosions in the air coming above all from the side of the general, who used weaponry as a powerful deterrent. Though the Romans weren't going to cave because of simple scare tactics. The proof? A week after the affair, at a point when both sides had so far contented themselves with trying to stare each other down, the Romans opened hostilities, taking advantage of a dark, rain-lashed night to launch a large-scale offensive around three in the morning, in a region in the southern part of the capital. Exchanges of fire shook the city—it was as if a dormant volcano had come to life and was making up in a single day for a century of sleep. The inhabitants felt like Mapapouville had been turned upside down, shaken, ground up by an immense monster who spat inextinguishable fire from its gaping mouth. That night the fighting intensified around the airport. The Anacondas and the Negro Grandsons were able to contain the Romans' attacks, but they wouldn't be able to hold out for very long. Huge numbers of reinforcements arrived from the north part of the capital on the general's side. The Anacondas and the Negro Grandsons came under fire from multiple directions. The townspeople kept watch to the sound of heavy submachine gun fire and the flashes of rockets that rent the darkness then faded toward the Vietongo River. The Romans had decided to push back the government forces as far from the downtown neighborhood as possible and to gradually cut into their territory. Their objective was precise: to extend their occupation zone and control Mapapouville International Airport. They succeeded: the attack was crowned for the general and his men by the capture of the television and radio stations, which were located in the same area. That was how the Okonongo Affair inflamed the country and led to the fall of President Lebou Kabouya! We know the rest: General Edou became master of Mapapouville and the whole of the North of the country. In the southern part of the city, the Negro Grandsons refuse to this day to recognize the general's authority. A general exodus of the government marked the end of five years in power for President Lebou Kabouya, who waited in vain for help from the international community and above all from other countries of this continent! I'm sure you know the story about how, only hours before he fled, President Lebou Kabouya asked his people: 'What became of Vercingetorix, who was supposed to give our troops the magic potion?'"

"They told him that the former prime minister was en route for the district of Batalébé with a contingent of his Negro Grandsons!"

"After this reply, His Excellency realized it was all over. The last group of those loyal to him crossed the river by night and gained the neighboring country. It's also said that His Excellency wept as he joined one of those crossings, under a hail of gunfire.

"The next day, without any further fighting, the general took possession of the presidential palace. The Vietongolese watched the fall of the southerners on television. The private residence of President Lebou Kabouya was razed to the ground. The Romans celebrated, firing in the air and dancing on the magnificent tables in the palace. Official photographs of His Excellency were peppered with bullets or were caricatured in southern blood, then replaced with pictures of the general."

Confusion in Mapapouville

I hadn't realized how well informed Christiane was about our current political situation. The day she spoke about the Oko-nongo Affair, I came to believe that Gaston must have been receiving up-to-date news from Mapapouville. The previous evening he must have spoken with his wife, explained recent developments to her. I envied that marital harmony, which contrasted with my own. In our household we never spoke a word

about politics, though Kimbembé had become involved in this
new activity.

To tell the truth, we no longer knew what had been happening in Mapapouville since the Okonongo Affair and the
flight of the southern president. All was confusion. Like other
Vietongolese, we were no longer able to pick up foreign radio
stations. The national radio told us nothing new. It restricted
itself to repeating over and over the official version and offering
a one-sided analysis. In Batalébé it was thought that the new
authorities in Mapapouville were jamming the frequencies
of overseas radio stations. We knew that those now in power
were no longer at ease, since they had decreed that listening
to foreign radio stations constituted a serious offense against
Vietongolese sovereignty. General Edou personally announced
that offenders would be labeled "local lackeys of the imperialists" and punished as such. They would receive a visit from
the Romans. During their three-month detention, aside from
being subjected to the most humiliating abuse, the "local
lackeys of the imperialists" would copy out our new national
anthem seventy-seven times, seven times a day. That was why
Kimbembé made sure our radio was permanently switched
off—it was a way of ignoring the authorities. The order handed
down by Vercingetorix was not to listen to the prevarications
of those in power, since they threatened to weaken the rebels' morale. This wasn't an empty argument: listening to the
national airwaves, you'd think the Romans had reached the
Moukoukoulou Dam and were gearing up for the final push.
"Confrontations can be won through public relations alone,"
Vercingetorix proclaimed to his Negro Grandsons. So above
all it was vital not to listen to what was said on the Voice of the
Vietongolese Revolution.

* * *

Yet I wished to have for myself an overall picture of national events. To know how the ideology of those in power had been propagated around the country. I would wait till my husband's back was turned, then tune in to one of the two Vietongolese stations. I'd lower the volume to the point that I had to hold the radio to one ear, the other listening out to make sure Kimbembé wasn't back.

When I ventured to ask him one day why he forbade us to listen to the national radio, he answered peremptorily that the president who had just taken power and the national authorities were destroying the integrity of Vietongo. They had no legitimacy, not having been elected by the people.

"Unless of course you're interested in hearing your brothers from the North, who have just seized power from us in such a shameful fashion."

II

The War of the Airwaves

Here in Louboulou I can listen to the Voice of the Vietongolese Revolution without being afraid. I was right in following
Christiane's advice not to forget the radio. I'm also interested in
the commentary on the foreign stations that I can now pick up.
I know that at the present moment the authorities will not tell
us everything. I can't imagine them divulging their intentions
and announcing the exact day and time of the final assault. So
I listen to Radio-Intercontinentale. It's easy to find, even out
here in the bush. Sometimes there's interference, but it doesn't
usually last long. Reception ends up being reasonable.

* * *

According to the most recent broadcasts on Radio-
Intercontinentale, the situation is getting worse. The station
reports that cleaning operations are going on in the outskirts
of Mapapouville, and in the weeks to come it's to be expected
that this will expand, with an intensive sweep of areas in the
South by the Romans and by units from neighboring countries
that have been sent as reinforcements to support the general,
the country's new strongman.

The information provided by the Voice of the Vietongolese
Revolution seems to unwittingly corroborate that of the foreign
station. Before, the presenters would speak in many different

languages, to the point that even southerners could understand the general's communiqués. Now they only use the languages of the North. Not being from that region myself, I only understand fifty percent of it. In fact the communiqués are couched in old dialects, those of our great-great-grandparents, which are no longer spoken except by those familiar with the farthest corners of the North, on the far bank of the Vietongo River, near the village where the general was born. These announcements are one-sided. But how can the listeners decode them if they're not in their own languages?

Actually the explanation is simple. The messages are ultimatums. Provocations. Intimidations. Theories about the natural superiority of northerners. This is nothing new. A long time ago the authorities launched an intimidation campaign over the airwaves. Although Kimbembé had kept urging me, back then I hadn't explained the meaning of what he referred to as the "gruntings of backward northerners." How could I have spoken to him about it without antagonizing him? Tension was mounting in the district. His Excellency Lebou Kabouya had already fled the presidential palace and crossed the river with his last remaining supporters. Kimbembé was no longer capable of listening to me, of giving me a few minutes of his attention, preoccupied as he was by his new activities as a committed militant in the region. He had chosen his path. After more than sixteen years of marriage, I no longer knew him. I was dumbfounded to realize it was possible to change like that from one day to the next. That still waters could produce the most tragic flood. I sometimes thought that perhaps I myself had acted badly. My opinion mattered little to him. He was no longer the same man who had fascinated me in the North, when he was a teacher of history, geography, and French at the Aimé Césaire Middle School. No, he wasn't the same man. He was a stranger. His gaze had become evasive, craven, and pathologically deceitful.

The events had affected him, like most of the inhabitants of the South.

Choosing Sides

In reality, and this is not to make excuses for him, Kimbembé too had been hit hard by the rout of President Lebou Kabouya. The whole of the South was plunged into darkness by the flight of "their" president. The southerners could hold all kinds of things against their leader, but he remained a man of the South, and he had to be supported so that power should remain in the hands of the region. Kimbembé, like other southerners, had experienced the overthrow as if it had been his own. His whole existence had been knocked off balance the moment the president fell. Plus, the foreign press had dwelled on His Excellency's last hours in Mapapouville before he crossed the river in a small boat, heading for one of Vietongo's neighbors. Kimbembé lost his appetite that day. Without any explanation, he warned me not to go to Christiane's anymore. Not to spend time with that pair of traitors. I had to stay at home.

"It's over with those people! Over, you hear? Over!" he raged.

"What's going on?" I asked innocently. "You've no right to call them 'those people'! Christiane and Gaston are our friends, and surely you always enjoyed Gaston's company when the two of you would—"

"I said it's over, period! They're not our friends. I won't tell you twice!"

"Then give me one good reason why I should stop seeing them."

"Go ahead and visit them, if you don't value your own life anymore!"

"You seem to have chosen sides, but you're forgetting that your daughter can't!"

"Be quiet! I know it's Christiane, that Judas, who's gotten to you with her claptrap! Don't let me find out you've taken my daughter there on top of everything else!"

Late in the afternoon he rushed out of the house toward the center of Batalébé, where a huge crowd, grieved by the fall of His Excellency Lebou Kabouya, had gathered to hear remarks and watchwords from the Negro Grandsons of Vercingetorix. The former prime minister himself was on his way to Batalébé, his loyal lieutenants assured everyone.

Marital Tensions

Did President Lebou Kabouya suffer as much as Kimbembé did? Even now I doubt it. In any case, the least word I uttered provoked him. I was supposed to remain completely silent on the subject or risk being called "a damn northerner." According to him, I was hiding my satisfaction at the change of regime, which at bottom was supposedly to my advantage. When he spoke of it, he implicated me.

"So there you all are, back in power, as usual, by machine guns!"

At those moments I kept my peace. I didn't give him an opportunity to start an argument on that subject. Having failed to fluster me, he would pace up and down, then flop into an armchair and leaf through the free Southernist propaganda newspaper that the Negro Grandsons put out in Batalébé. After that he would turn on the radio, tuning in to the stations he wouldn't let me listen to. The Voice of the Vietongolese Revolution, or Radio Liberté. It would be General Edou speaking. Or rather, his speech from two days before, which they were repeating. His eyes red with anger, Kimbembé would soon switch the thing off, suppressing the urge to punch the radio set. He'd sit huffing by the window, glancing at the mass of buildings that we could see from our house on the hill, which was somewhat apart from other dwellings. He would straighten his Dutch wax jacket, tugging sharply at the lapels. He'd slam the door, and I'd see him striding down the hill and along the main road leading to the center of Batalébé. I knew he'd be holding discussions with Vercingetorix's men. And in these talks, the pitch would rise as each man laid out his view of things, taking the former prime minister's words as his point of reference. Their debates, which would turn into disputes and even fisticuffs, would go on till one or two in the morning. Everyone was trying to predict the date of Vercingetorix's return to the district. He had nothing more to do in Mapapouville, they agreed. He would be more effective in his native region than elsewhere. They couldn't imagine him opting for exile in Europe, the way His Excellency had when he lost the election.

Nights of Humiliation

When Kimbembé came back home, he'd resume his attacks. He'd mutter insults aimed at the "northern dogs." With his sudden changes of mood every day, he made me feel as if it were my father who had come to power. As if I knew General Edou personally. I concluded that the only sin I'd committed was being a northerner. As if he had only just brought that to light.

But more than anything, there are other images that come back to me. And here I immediately feel the same sense of repugnance as the day those things happened. It was often very late at night, when Maribé was asleep on the other side of the house. I'd record such moments in my notebooks the next day, after Kimbembé went out.

In the night, I would barely have closed my eyes when I'd feel a shadow approaching and reaching out as if to take me by surprise. It was him, Kimbembé. He no longer knew how to proceed. It was no longer easy for him, the more so because he sensed a lack of engagement on my part. Yes, I knew he wanted to touch me on those nights. But he had to do it like a thief, even if he was sure that I wouldn't protest, that I'd let it happen, that my body was now nothing more than a hollow trunk eaten away by the burden of doubt. Kimbembé would go at it with mechanical, clumsy movements. The feel of his hands on my skin disgusted me. Perhaps he noticed the gooseflesh that came from my unease. I felt sullied, treated as an object. I would tense up because he took me without any ado, with a deliberate brutishness, as if he wanted to get it over with as quickly as possible and escape from the remorse that would come to haunt him. As he found his release, twitching back and forth, I wished only for one thing—that he would unfasten himself from me quickly.

A Portrait of Vercingetorix in Our Home

In fact, Kimbembé had ceased to be at all approachable from the time he'd started associating with Vercingetorix and his Negro Grandsons. People in Batalébé said that when my husband had spoken in the Palaver House for the first time, he'd made a good impression on the rebel of the South. Vercingetorix had found him insightful and intelligent and had decided to entrust him with all the paperwork. Kimbembé ran the office and wrote up the minutes of the meetings in the Palaver House.

One evening, some time after Vercingetorix had come to the district of Batalébé, I was presented with a fait accompli. Kimbembé came home early with some kind of framed object wrapped in brown paper. When he opened it, as I was crossing the dining room on my way to Maribé's bedroom, I saw that it was a huge portrait of the southern rebel. An image of Vercingetorix affecting a pensive stance, his right hand under his chin.

Kimbembé climbed onto a chair to attach the photograph to the wall near the window. A few minutes later he decided that wasn't the right place. He took it down and moved it closer to the dining table. So now the former prime minister was living with us, in the same house. Whenever I found myself in the dining room, Vercingetorix was watching me, following me with his eyes.

Maribé noticed it too, saying: "He never laughs, and he never stops looking this way!"

The picture bothered both of us, and it was hard for me to explain to Maribé who this man was—she had taken him to be a relative on her father's side. It was one of the few times I spoke to her about those things.

I only grasped the meaning of Kimbembé's zeal a week later, when the leader of the South paid him a visit, accompanied by his bodyguards. A Peugeot 504 with tinted windows pulled up right in front of our house. Vercingetorix was preceded by two armed men with oily, sinister faces. My husband had not told me about this visit beforehand. Of course, I'd been able to see Vercingetorix when he gave a speech on the market square on the occasion of his return to the district after the fall of President Lebou Kabouya. Now I saw him close up. Behind his seeming affability I discerned a duplicity that seemed to gouge furrows in his face. He stared at me as if I were an object that was out of place. In fact, he didn't say a word to me after he had shaken my hand indifferently. Kimbembé invited him in and gestured toward a chair. The former prime minister sat down facing his own portrait, though for several minutes he gave the impression of not having noticed it. In the end he alluded to it at the moment when I was putting two glasses and a bottle of corn liquor on the table before going back to Maribé outside.

"My dear Kimbembé," Vercingetorix said, raising his glass, "how can you bear having my twin in front of you all the time?"

"Prime Minister, it's an honor for me to have him in my home, and I hope he won't be jealous of your presence here today."

Vercingetorix took some files out of his briefcase and donned his reading glasses.

I don't know what was said after that. Their tête-à-tête lasted over an hour. The bodyguards paced up and down outside, crushing their cigarette butts with their heels. They hurried toward the Peugeot 504 when Vercingetorix reappeared, followed by Kimbembé. After a long handshake between the two men, the vehicle swept away as we stood there.

After that visit, whenever Kimbembé opened his mouth in the house, it almost seemed like I was hearing Vercingetorix in person, on the market square, with his legendary diatribes and his overdone, third-rate actor's gestures.

The Rally

Before his visit to our house, I'd seen Vercingetorix once before at a rally, after his return to Batalébé. Naturally we used to see him on television, especially after he was appointed prime minister by President Lebou Kabouya.

The rally marking his return took place on the market square—the Palaver House was no longer adequate, given the growing numbers of his supporters.

I stood apart from the crowd, lurking behind a block of houses. The echoing sounds from the loudspeakers filled the area, and I didn't need to go any closer to hear the speech clearly. My choice of place could have cost me dearly if I'd been discovered by Kimbembé or one of his acquaintances. I'd taken the risk, and I was certain that Christiane too was somewhere around, perhaps half-hidden like me. I wanted to finally see this Vercingetorix, to hear him for real. He had left a mark on the inhabitants of Batalébé, and on others in the South too. First, because he had managed to convince them that they belonged to "one of the most glorious ethnic groups on the continent," to quote his words. After that, as a seasoned sophist he had emphatically shown that the defeat of His Excellency Lebou Kabouya was not the defeat of the entire South. President Lebou Kabouya was a man, he said, who had "foolishly" lost power. It had been the downfall of an individual, not of the South as a whole.

At each of the rallies in the market square, the crowd came running, begging for his words and his analysis of events, for he had seen everything from the inside, in Mapapouville. He had fought the general and his Romans in the heart of the capital. And now as he spoke, he knew how to use all the right words, the most poignant images, the most thrilling incidents from the history of Vietongo. He invoked the heroes of his ethnic group. Those endowed with Herculean strength, who in spite of themselves had helped the colonist in constructing the Mapapouville-Pointe-Rouge railroad. And above all, those who could make themselves invisible at a snap of the fingers or shoot down their foe with nothing but kernels of corn fired from a shotgun.

Vercingetorix was influential nationwide. He'd appeared several times in foreign newspapers like *Le Monde*, *Libération*, and *Le Figaro*, pictured with white politicians who had never held power in their own country and who spent their entire lives criticizing those in government. Vercingetorix had not only denounced the successive political regimes in Vietongo. He was also implicated in them. In order to install himself as prime minister during the reign of His Excellency Lebou Kabouya, Vercingetorix had had to offer concessions—he who had always maintained an image as an oppositionist, a champion of rebellion, something he was fond of repeating. He had known prison. He boasted of it as proof of his tenacity and the purity of his beliefs. He had mentioned it during the speech he made upon returning to Batalébé. Everyone listening had been moved. Many people shed tears. The Negro Grandsons fired their guns in the air, braced by the optimism of the former prime minister.

His speech has remained in my head like a refrain:

For months upon months, for years upon years, I slept with cockroaches, rats, scorpions. I ate those creatures raw, just as they were eating me. My skin has become so hard that even bullets cannot penetrate it. I'm not in politics for the sake of a career, you know me well. I fight so the South should be free to express itself—from the tiniest embryo in the belly of a humble mother, to the bedridden old man whose days are uncertain. We are not cursed, and we shall show it one day. Yet waiting is not the solution: it was waiting that left the toad without a tail for all time.

No! We will wait no longer. I want my people, those of this region, to occupy the place that is theirs. In my political life I was asked to take part in several coups d'état, but I fiercely rejected the dagger that was held out to me. I cannot tolerate bloodshed, unlike many politicians you know. Today, I tell you, this country is in danger of being tossed in the rapids. The forces of night have reemerged to plunge us into the abyss. Are we going to accept that? I ask you, my brothers and my sisters! It's a matter of life and death. Should we allow General Edou's Romans to throw us to the lions? Let me tell you, no soul in the South will be spared if we let the Romans carry out the Machiavellian plan they're presently plotting from Mapapouville. Let us apply to the letter the resolutions we have agreed on that are in the best interest of the region and have been conveyed to all militants during meetings at the Palaver House.

The Story of Vercingetorix the Gaul

I daresay that as of today we are still in the South, far from Pointe-Rouge. I haven't forgotten that Batalébé and its environs are of particular interest to the authorities in Mapapouville. I sense the motives that drive General Edou: Batalébé is the birthplace of Vercingetorix; it is the electoral stronghold that previously carried His Excellency Lebou Kabouya to power.

The fact that the South should be a particular target of the general and his Romans did not trouble Vercingetorix and his Negro Grandsons. They were used to the intimidations of the

Mapapouville authorities. The chief rebel has increased the frequency of rallies in the district. He is rousing his lieutenants.

On the day of that first rally, I had a chance to gauge his personal charisma. It was also then that I heard him claim to be the true Vercingetorix and go so far as to declare that Batalébé and its surrounding area were like Gaul. These territories would never fall into the hands of Mapapouville's Romans, he proclaimed. I confess it was the first time I'd heard of the real Vercingetorix the Gaul, and I wasn't the only one, judging from the murmurs that followed the mention of that name. Many people had difficulty pronouncing it and thought Vercingetorix must be another hero of this continent, in the mold of Shaka Zulu. No, Vercingetorix was not a Black, the former prime minister went on, sowing doubt in the minds of his listeners.

Our ignorance was excusable. At school we had learned only the history of Vietongo and of Africa, in accordance with the "authenticity programs" that most rulers on the continent had introduced. Since we'd become independent, we no longer studied the history of France.

"Do the French study *our* history? What do they know about us? That our continent contains nothing but snakes, panthers, epidemics, and mosquitoes as big as sugar cubes!" the speaker thundered, egged on by lengthy applause.

So then, for a long time now the history of France had been banished from the school curriculum. At most, the abuse practiced by the White colonists might be highlighted. How they were described to us, those Whites! They were portrayed as desecrators of our customs and ways, our fetishes and totems; or as greedy bogeymen ogling our natural resources, which could be scooped up without even digging. And the former prime minister depicted the Whites of that period as carnivores moving about their colonies, enriching themselves through plunder, extortion, rape, while horsewhipping the poor, smiling, carefree Negroes. The White men were not white by chance, he went on, wiping his bulging forehead. God had made them that way to hide their hypocrisy from the eyes of the Blacks.

"They smile at you by day and stab you in the night, while your eyes are closed. They cut down our forests. They disturbed the sleep of our spirits in the bush. They dug down to the very depths of our resources. They chose our most beautiful women as playthings, blow-up dolls, flea hunters, automata waving flies away for the well-being of the little colonist. And let's talk about those colonists!" he bellowed, raising his fist in the air, his white shirt soaked with perspiration. "Nothings, less than nothings! Let me tell you what they were in reality. They fell over one another competing in colonial exoticism. Collectors of elephant tusks. Cowards, deserters from a war that was setting their snowbound continent ablaze. The same yellowbellies who later came looking for our help when they found themselves up against a pygmy Nazi who terrorized them simply by waggling his mustache in his office! And the Blacks, nothing but a bunch of sheep since the beginning of the world, went en masse to the slaughter. What did they get for it? Medals, tombs, impotents, cripples, nothing more. The Black is born that way. He gives the impression of deserving his own curse. For a medal he'll deliver up his mother as ground beef to the first freebooter who comes wandering through his territory. And on top of everything he'll do it with a big smile."

Thus spoke Ta Kanda, the former prime minister, who the entire country called Vercingetorix.

The Untold Defeat of the Leader of the Gauls

The day after Vercingetorix's harsh speech, I did some research in the Church Fathers library at the Church of Saint-Jean-Bosco opposite the town hall. The name *Vercingetorix* had been puzzling me all night. Having trusted the former prime minister's rendering, I imagined a tall, strong hero, with golden-blond hair and a full mustache, whose fearful sharp sword had repulsed entire columns of the Roman army.

I found out bit by bit that our national Vercingetorix had cut short the epic of the real Vercingetorix, chieftain of the Arverni. In fact, he had only spoken of the Vercingetorix who had been victorious at Gergovia. That episode suited his needs. In his speech he had explained the bold military stratagem he'd employed, destroying the bridges on the Allier River so as to undermine Julius Caesar, the Roman emperor. This legendary Vercingetorix, he had further explained, during his revolt in 52 BC had been able to unite all the Gaulish peoples under him in the fight against Caesar. In union there would be strength. What lesson were we in Vietongo supposed to take from this? That those in the South would have no chance if they did not unite against General Edou's Romans. It was quite something: our Vercingetorix recounting in his solemn, husky voice how Vercingetorix the Gaul, in order to get the better of Caesar, had come up with an ingenious ruse, ordering most of his men to high ground while he and his sappers remained lying in wait in the forest. The former prime minister had, like the real Vercingetorix, concluded that given the choice between a war of position and one of movement, the former was to be preferred. "Something that Julius Caesar learned at his own expense," he had said in finishing, making no effort to hide the satisfaction that showed on his face when the crowd was overcome by the breadth of his knowledge.

At that moment there was a storm of applause. The name of Vercingetorix was chanted. People raged against the Romans of Mapapouville and their Julius Caesar, General Edou, who in the end would yield in a war of position, not one of movement, which the Negro Grandsons would set in motion.

Vercingetorix the Gaul had become a model for the former prime minister in his speeches. Anyone who heard him would think that the chieftain of the Arverni had never experienced defeat. I knew now that he had surrendered and thrown his arms at the feet of Julius Caesar during the siege of Alesia. I also knew he had been executed after six years of captivity. The former prime minister had skillfully erased that chapter from his account, leaving the marveling crowd with an image of a mythic, invincible hero.

IV

The Wrap Dress Given to Mam'Soko

I listen more and more to the radio, even while I'm writing these lines. I sometimes tell myself that perhaps I'm writing to kill time during the wait, which weighs on our shoulders. Yes, I write so as to bring our departure closer.

Daybreak comes, and there I am, sitting, my nose in my notebooks. Sometimes I fall asleep—my pallet is right next to me. It takes an effort even to look out the window at the plants waking up. I go down into the orchard to pick a handful of fruit. I also take vegetables. My daughter knows how to cook, and she prepares the dish we'll eat. We set aside a plate, which Maribé takes over to Mam'Soko.

I no longer notice the old lady moving to and fro behind our house. From time to time Maribé wanders outside and joins her in the orchard. That comforts me. She's getting used to this place.

The other day, Maribé went to wash the old lady's dusty wrap dresses in the river. Mam'Soko protested. She thought it was a waste of time; she said she no longer attached any importance to such everyday chores. Why should she wash her clothes?

"After all, we're nothing but dust! It's too bad—instead of just living with it, we spend our lives sweeping it away, hunting it down, pushing it from ourselves, only to return to it, against our will, the day we die."

Coming back from the river, Maribé spread out Mam'Soko's clothes on the grass alongside the house to dry.

Clothes? Rags, rather. Old styles in Dutch wax. From among our things I took out a new wrap dress, which I gave to the old lady. She examined it curiously. I knew she could no longer tell colors apart. That was why she spent a long time feeling the garment. She smiled. All at once her face lit up. She was thinking about something. She tapped her cane three times on the ground. That meant she was thanking us for the gift.

Yet up to now she hasn't used the new wrap. When I tried to insist that she put it on, she answered calmly: "I'll wear it in the next world. On that day, I'll make myself beautiful for my husband, Massengo. For him alone. He'll be surprised to see me coming, walking through the clouds, with angel's wings."

The Warning

The bulletins put out on national radio are military orders barked by zealous journalists who support General Edou's cause. I listen for hours as the general speaks in a monotone. The radio cannot restrict itself to broadcasting only extracts from these "messages to the nation." The president is not to be interrupted while he's talking. On what basis would a journalist permit himself to select the most important passages from the head of state's speeches? Everything he says is good and useful, even if he's talking gibberish.

In his broadcasts the general repeats that there will be no compromises. That this is no longer the time for speeches or for forgiveness. That he has returned to politics to decontaminate the country, to "sweep clean the house of Vietongo, in front of which there is a pile of refuse, growing daily, that prevents the people from breathing." It's his duty, that of the commander in chief of our army. "So then, the Negro Grandsons of Vercingetorix are wrong to think of themselves as unconquerable Gauls," he says. You can hear him hammering his fist on the table. He calls on the southern rebels to listen to the voice of reason, to lay down their arms unconditionally and give themselves up. He even promises to incorporate those rebels who surrender into the national army, and not to prosecute the offenders and criminals in the South. He says nothing on the subject of Vercingetorix, holed up in Batalébé, or His Excellency Lebou Kabouya, who is in exile in Europe.

Christiane's Advice

Vercingetorix did not come to the house again. Christiane and I discussed his surprise visit, which had made my husband so happy. We were in the middle of the crowd in the marketplace. The way people looked at us had changed. We'd realized that our friendship bothered the local residents. Yet Christiane remained a lifeline to me. Her presence comforted me.

Right up until our departure, I ignored Kimbembé's prohibition. I continued to see my old friend. What reason could I have given Christiane for no longer visiting her? Of course, Christiane thoughtfully put herself in my place.

She cautioned me: "I think we need to stop meeting. Your husband is aware that we spend time together."

"I'm not going to give in to his cowardice," I retorted.

"It's not a question of cowardice, Hortense. It's not for nothing that Vercingetorix came to your place: he wanted to see you in person."

"Me?"

"Yes, a bit like the way a criminal checks out his next victim. If he'd wanted to work undisturbed with your husband, he'd have summoned him to the Palaver House. From now on, get used to the idea that you have only one solution: to leave the district the first chance that presents itself. Believe me, I know what that man is capable of."

V

Mapapouville Blues

Today I'm prey to a certain nostalgia. I don't know why I can't stop thinking of our capital. I have moments like this, when my thoughts wander independently of me.

I'm seeing the city again. From here I can dive back into its streets, its depths, into the soul of the place, which has gone to pieces since the Okonongo Affair.

Mapapouville was a huge metropolis famed throughout the continent despite the contrast between its various neighborhoods. Political, cultural, and religious capital, it was known as the Green City thanks to its greenery: the flame trees lining its avenues, its public gardens, the flower-covered roundabouts, and the fountains from which doves with golden plumage would rise into the air. The downtown area, once the European city, housed government offices, large businesses, and services. Towers of glass. Multistory housing. Reinforced concrete bridges. The architecture had been modeled on the West, and it contrasted sharply with other parts of the city—to the south especially there was a multitude of lively residential quarters with countless children in motion, always outside, on the public squares, in the dead-end streets, or in the passages that ran between private properties. The same urchins could be seen in front of the stalls of sidewalk sellers, when they weren't chasing after a moped or some aging automobile.

If today everything has been demolished, the fact remains that our capital still extends along the bank of the Vietongo River, like a vast boa constrictor sleeping off a filling meal.

The expansion of the city led to the appearance of myriad outlying neighborhoods, unsurveyed, with bamboo huts and shacks of plywood or aluminum sheeting, that ringed the center closely on stretches of land as diverse as plains, ravines, and plateaus. In the places still covered with trees, electricity was lacking. When night fell, these favela-like constructions were plunged in darkness. From time to time a flashlight, the headlights of a moped or car, or a hurricane lamp would reveal the existence of the souls huddling in those places.

Forgotten Splendor

Today I find it impossible to believe that Mapapouville was once a mélange of ethnic groups. Men and women from different regions, all brought together. A conglomeration of origins sharing the city. This world was jumbled up, mixed together in the markets, the factories, the buses, the stations, the restaurants and bars. Here you forgot the mud of your native village, the customs of your region, your local accent. A particular tribe was no longer denounced because they liked the meat of dogs or cats; another because they had a weakness for spicy shark soup, monkey, or gorilla; a third because they were keen on grasshoppers or caterpillars, to be eaten with large chunks of cassava and a big tumbler of cool water. At these moments of mingling, of the crowd, a different culture emerged—an urban culture that was composite and hybrid. People clinked glasses together. They helped old ladies carry their bags, cross the road, or get around a puddle. They let the skinny bald old man have their seat on public transportation and gave him directions when he got off. People spoke one of the country's two official languages, French and Lingala, so the different tribes could understand each other better. The same restaurant in the neighborhood or at the market would serve dog, cat, gorilla, and monkey. There were dishes of boa and of palm rat. Shark was also available, and you could comfortably order any number of grasshoppers from the Mayombe forest and grilled caterpillars from the Dziama grasslands. And when the beer flowed—yes, real beer, not the stuff they drink today, but a well-chilled beer that lingered on the palate to the point that it made your tongue click, filled your throat, slipped down your gullet—well, when that beer flowed, no one knew anymore which tribe ate what, and all hands dipped in all the different dishes being served. On a single table there'd be empty bottles of chilled Kronenbourg, Primus, or Ngok, the local beer. Then there were the older folks, with their long bottle of red wine. They'd come into the bar and ask for a Sonvico long, or the half long they'd not been able to finish the night before and had set aside.

The Mapapouvillians forgot their differences and their customs during these moments of jubilation and intermingling. The ethnic organization of the city was anchored in our traditions, and it extended to many facets of everyday life.

* * *

I say to myself now that Mapapouville was like our soccer teams from that time. Because like other big cities of our continent, our political capital was prey to football fever. Every game was a national event. The Revolution Stadium would fill up early in the morning, even though kickoff wasn't till late afternoon. The makeup of the teams showed the point to which tribal identity was set in people's minds. A. S. Kilahou consisted of players, a coach, and managers from the South of the country. A. S. Bokondima, on the other hand, was the team of the North, from their physio to their fan club, including the administration and the sponsors. A few teams from the central region and from little towns had walk-on parts in the national championship. Do I need to stress how the entire country would be in a turmoil of excitement when Bokondima faced Kilahou? It was obviously a contest between northerners and southerners. In other words, between those who were in power and those who were not. The city would grind to a halt during this confrontation. Traffic came to a standstill. The bars were packed; people would sit around a big wooden radio set, a colonial fossil, that was so dilapidated the listeners constantly had to take turns, between the referee's whistles, at turning the antenna so they could follow the spirited and partisan commentaries by the two official sports journalists (one northerner and one southerner).

This idyllic image contrasts sharply with the analysis I heard the day before yesterday on Radio-Intercontinentale, summing up the events in Mapapouville. According to that station, the city has been nothing but a dead house since General Edou and his Romans laid siege to it. The broadcast added that the legitimate regime of His Excellency Lebou Kabouya was smashed to pieces after a coup d'état in which the general was implicated. The deposed president's Anacondas have vanished into the scenery. Some of them became turncoats and laid down their arms at the feet of the new strongman of Mapapouville. Only the Negro Grandsons, loyal to the southern former prime minister Vercingetorix, are still in place in the poorer districts of the capital, making life difficult for the putschists. But they are being pushed back by the Romans, who have the advantage of aid from Vietongo's neighbors. General Edou has become sole master of the country. In the South, the radio confirmed, the Negro Grandsons are refusing to recognize the general's authority, and it has been established that at present Vercingetorix is back in Batalébé, his native district. He has decided to remind the general that his men are heroes and that they will not spare any northerner living in the South of the country.

VI

The Return of Vercingetorix to Batalébé

With the return of Vercingetorix to Batalébé, we understood that the events of Mapapouville were now going to affect our region. It was at this time that Christiane began to alert me to danger. It was no longer possible to go anywhere in the district without encountering the Negro Grandsons in military uniform. The southerners had organized for resistance. Meetings took place in the Palaver House. The first measure that Vercingetorix had instituted was a hunt for northerners.

* * *

Since then the Negro Grandsons have been looking for "traitors," meaning northerners who reside in the South. Vercingetorix has vowed to scalp them and send their skulls to General Edou.

Gaston Okemba was one of the first guinea pigs for this furious operation. Working at the Moukoukoulou Dam had been enough for him to be singled out at the beginning. And the Negro Grandsons had carried out their leader's instructions to the letter.

* * *

A few days before we fled, I saw the leaflets that Vercingetorix's men were distributing in the schools, calling for rallies and for the defense of southern interests. In the Palaver House many speakers had inveighed against His Excellency Lebou Kabouya, the "bad southerner" who had caused the region to fall from power. The motivational speech that Vercingetorix gave on the market square poisoned the atmosphere in the South.

> I say to you, and I will not tire of saying to you: we have not lost the war, we have only lost the battle, in the words of General de Gaulle. The South will present an implacable resistance to those who recently took power in Mapapouville. We are in the majority. We have the oil! We have the sea! All the great intellectuals of this country are southerners! The northerners have nothing but forests. We will not allow ourselves to be crushed by peasants who have muscles and submachine guns in place of brains! No! In addition, it must be said that we lost power in a foolish way. President Lebou Kabouya was guilty of inexcusable weakness. He did not listen to his own people, he did whatever he wanted. Why did he let General Edou return from exile in Europe and parade about with his Romans in the capital? Why did he not lock him up on the spot? And there he was, His Excellency Lebou Kabouya, talking to us about freedom of movement, freedom of speech! Now we must act. We must ask ourselves the question that Lenin himself asked in his time: What is to be done? It is precisely for that reason that I have decided to return here instead of going into exile in Europe like the rest. The general wants my hide? Let him come here for it; he shouldn't count on me handing it to him on a silver platter!
>
> What is to be done? Time is pressing. We have to put together a list of northerners living in our region. We have to know what they do, what they think, what they eat, what they read, who they spend time with. I want this task to be our day-to-day priority. Let us not forget that treason can come from anywhere. It is here, in our ranks, in our homes. We will fight so our children should never say that we went down on our knees before these northerners, these sons of dugout boatmen

and fishermen, these people with no railroad, no sea, and
no oil!

What is to be done? Do not fear the bombardment that those
in power are threatening. The northerners are afraid of crossing the Moukoukoulou Dam. For them, this region is what
Diên Biên Phu was for France. We know the country better—
its lakes, its rivers, its swamps. We will be able to surprise our
attackers by employing the stratagems used by Vercingetorix
against Julius Caesar. I tell you we are all Negro Grandsons
of Vercingetorix! Victory awaits us. We will be invincible,
mystical, mighty. Our dead will rise up from their graves with
their assegais that are faster than missiles. The trees will march
in the nighttime, lashing the faces of our enemies with their
branches in revolt. And twelve-headed monsters will burst
forth from the depths of the rivers, along with green mambas
and other snakes thick as the trunk of a baobab.

What is to be done? Strength has always been on our side,
my dear brothers and sisters. Remember the confrontations
of the fifties, when we went all the way to Mfoa to the res-
cue of our brothers and sisters of the South in danger from
northerners, on whom we had inflicted a historic defeat. Such
courage! Such incredible courage! That is the courage we have
need of today. In that historic battle, among our ranks was a
man to whom I must pay public tribute. His name was Moussahou. He was nimble. He was able to fly, to single-handedly
disrupt the forces of the enemy. In the midst of the fray, he
found himself face to face with a group of men armed to the
teeth who were closing in on him. You will not believe me, but
their bullets bounced off his chest without so much as scratch-
ing him. Moussahou moved forward, straight ahead, glaring
at the northerners, who dropped their weapons and fled! Our
hero snatched up a shotgun and loaded it with corn kernels.
The gunfire that followed made Mfoa shake. He killed dozens
of the enemy with each shot.

What is to be done? My dear brothers and sisters, the illegit-
imate authorities of Mapapouville have set their minds on
annihilating our region, on wiping out anything that breathes.

On the scale of barbarity, this is no longer slaughter but out-right genocide. Let us not be afraid of words! From this day on, I call upon my fellow countrymen to hunt down any northern-ers living in our territory, to bring their scalps and drop them at my feet. They are the ones who are selling us out to their broth-ers. Everything we say here in Batalébé is reported in detail in Mapapouville by these traitors, who are eating us away from the inside. I no longer wish to provide for those who take the side of the executioner. Above all I point to those of our broth-ers who have committed the blunder of marrying women of the North, to our sisters who are living with northern men. This is a matter of life and death! Do not place personal inter-est over the cause of the region. Without knowing it, you are harboring vermin that will gnaw at your dead body. I charge you to live up to your responsibilities.

The Internment Camp

The hunt for northerners was on. Vercingetorix's words echoed throughout the South, peddled from lips to ears. There were settlings of scores on every street corner. Gratuitous murders. Looting, destruction of personal property. A marriage between a northerner and a southerner? Treachery! Mixed couples were publicly torn apart. After the separation, the northerner was delivered into the hands of the Negro Grandsons, who took him or her to an internment camp deep in the bush. Some couples had resisted, love becoming their only shield against the poisoned arrows of zealots.

The example of Gaston and Christiane remained with me.

The Woman Prisoner and Her Child

In Batalébé we knew that the Romans were doing the same thing as the Negro Grandsons, in turn persecuting southerners who lived in Mapapouville.

Two weeks after she had explained the Okonongo Affair to me, Christiane told me of the ordeal suffered by a southern woman who lived in Mapapouville. Mother of a small baby, she had been pointed out to the Romans as being a first cousin of Vercingetorix. She denied this family connection, which was being wrongly ascribed to her. She didn't know Vercingetorix. She had never seen him close up. She swore this by the child in her arms. As a witness she called on another southerner detained in the same building, who was from the same village as her. Yet this witness, a small red-eyed man, bald and dark skinned, claimed not to know the woman, never to have seen her in his life. The woman, outraged, gave the name of this man who could not remember anything. Without hesitation she further revealed the names of his mother, his grandparents, and some of his cousins. The Romans now turned their attention to the man. He was sweating, passing his hand over his head, which a merciless premature baldness had left with only wisps of gray hair around the ears. Taken aback, the southerner mumbled some indistinct words. After a moment in which he revealed his nervousness by cracking his fingers, he denied it once again, shaking his head three times as a sign of absolute negation.

"No, no, no! I don't know this woman. I'm not from her village. And she doesn't know me either. She's lying!"

On hearing his words, the Romans left him alone. He had just saved his own skin. Rage filled the woman's chest. She spat a thick mouthful of saliva in the face of the coward and spoke to him in Bembé, a language that the general's soldiers could not understand. One of the Romans demanded a translation from another prisoner, who had been the only one to approve of the southern woman's words.

"This brave woman was telling the forgetful man to make sure his balls haven't disappeared from his pants after all his lies and denials."

The claim made by the bald southerner was about to have grave consequences. If he's still alive, I'm certain that the memory of that accursed day will keep coming back to him and will prevent him from sleeping for the rest of his life.

The Romans, convinced that the woman was related to Vercingetorix, intensified their mistreatment. The woman held the baby tightly to her chest and tried to calm it. For the last time the Romans advised her to admit the relation.

She denied it once again.

"I'm not his cousin. I'm from the same region and the same tribe as him, and also as this man with no hair and no courage who has betrayed the pride of his ancestors. If Vercingetorix were a relative of mine, I'd be proud to admit it to anyone, in any circumstances!"

One of the Romans, infuriated by this talk, grabbed the baby from its mother's arms. The other soldiers watched dumbfounded. The Roman ordered a large mortar and pestle to be brought. In a couple of minutes these objects were laid at his feet. The baby bawled as the soldier shook it, holding it upside down in one hand. With a rapid, precise movement, he dropped the crying baby in the mortar and snatched up the pestle, which he raised high above his head, ignoring the stunned cries of the detainees pinned against the wall. The Roman backed up a little, set his jaw, and closed his eyes before bringing the pestle down with a powerful blow that knocked the tiny naked body of the baby to the bottom of the bowl. The last cry uttered by the child was stifled in its throat, at the moment when the mother flung herself with all her remaining strength on the Roman executioner, who smacked her with the back of his hand.

The woman collapsed unconscious.

Kimbembé's Silence

Kimbembé went to the Palaver House every evening. He prepared for these meetings at home, very late, in front of the portrait of Vercingetorix. Deep down I still had faith in him. He wasn't capable of handing me over to his people, despite the urgings of the former prime minister. He would spare me, I told myself. Our shared past would win out over the extremist fervor that had gripped the men of the district. Kimbembé would think above all of our marriage, of our daughter, Maribé. I reassured myself by imagining that he had forbidden me to visit Christiane in order to protect me. I'd be safer at home close to my daughter. That was it.

And then, a month later, came the arrest and internment of Gaston Okemba, and Christiane's humiliation. I no longer believed in Kimbembé. He couldn't rub shoulders with these monsters. He couldn't endorse their ideas. He couldn't have allowed a man like Gaston to fall into the hands of the Negro Grandsons of Vercingetorix. True, he had no power of decision. But he could at least have reacted, shown me he was shocked, outraged by these actions. There hadn't been one word of regret, not one mention of the arrest. It had all seemed normal to him. Gaston could die; it didn't bother him at all.

So I continued to disobey his orders. I'd been to see Christiane a week after the misfortune that had befallen her. I couldn't visit sooner, as I knew Kimbembé was watching me like a hawk.

I wanted to get news of Christiane, to learn more about Gaston. I wanted to hear about the tragedy from her own lips, in her words and her voice, with her repetitions. I wanted to sit down on the mat by the window and listen to her all afternoon. From now on I couldn't have cared less if I'd been caught entering their yard.

VII

An Atmosphere of Suspicion

I hadn't slept since Vercingetorix's speech calling for northerners to be hunted. *When will my turn come?* I worried every night. I had dreams of Kimbembé turning up at the house, followed by the Negro Grandsons.

In the district it was common knowledge that he had a northern wife. Why had I not quickly shared Gaston's fate? Christiane could see clearly: it was because Kimbembé had become an active participant in their cause. But how long would the grace period last? The Negro Grandsons would make their minds up one day or another.

Fear was creeping over me. Christiane alone could speak to me, tell me what was right for my daughter and me. She had heard rumors about Kimbembé and me. Kimbembé was under pressure from the Negro Grandsons. He'd had to promise them that he would personally take care of things, though discreetly. It wasn't easy for him. I hadn't done anything to him. Nor had my daughter. How should he proceed? By provocations, changes of mood. I did not respond, for I sensed the consequences. I was cooped up in the house with Maribé. Certain signs made me think: for example, when Kimbembé watched closely to see what I was cooking. I had to taste the dish before him. He was afraid of being poisoned. We no longer made love. Except the times he would grab hold of me, or surprise me as

I slept, pushing me and turning me over. Face tense and lips shut tight, he concentrated on his task. The next day, without a word, he would leave again for the Palaver House to talk with the district elders before busying himself getting supplies to the rebels hiding in the forest. He had stopped working because salaries had ceased to be paid since the events in Mapapouville. He didn't even read anymore the way he used to when I met him. He got up in the morning, went out without washing, and met up with his fellows in the cause.

I knew he could no longer be reasoned with when he took it out on his daughter for the first time. Maribé had gone to the center of Batalébé with a school friend. Informers had let my husband know that the parents of the friend in question were northerners. That was true, though I didn't know the family; it seemed they came from Onzoto, a district in the North. Maribé kept company with their daughter, who incidentally never came to our house. On that day Kimbembé raised his voice, insulting his daughter in vulgar, indecent words. Maribé fled to her bedroom. Kimbembé forced the door open and dragged Maribé out into the living room by the arm. Snatching down a large spoon that hung on the wall, he hit her, hit her again. Maribé threw herself toward me, begging for help, though she knew she couldn't count on it. The blows that Kimbembé landed on her wounded me too. Every sob from my little girl broke my heart. I tried to step in, offering my body in place of our daughter's. He gave me a kick in the belly. I doubled over, then collapsed on the ground next to Maribé. Our tears kept coming. He called us "descendants of brutes who only knew how to handle a canoe or an assegai."

VIII

To Leave Batalébé at Any Cost

To go. Leave Batalébé. From then on this thought obsessed me. I was permanently prey to anxiety. I felt I was suffocating, dying by inches in this godforsaken place that had turned into a trap for northerners. The sky was hatching a tragedy whose fatal day was unknown to me. Christiane's warnings were well founded. She asked me what I intended to do. She kept urging me to run away with my daughter. I procrastinated.

And then the idea came home to me. Yes, I had to leave. We had to leave. How? In which direction? At what moment? I had to speak about it with Christiane as soon as possible. Preferably when Kimbembé would not be around.

The opportunity had presented itself. It remained only for me to pay a last visit to Christiane. To talk it over with her.

It was a farewell visit. She knew it. True, she didn't talk long, but deep down she knew that I was reading her thoughts about life in Pointe-Rouge, Gaston's abduction.

I listened to her. I didn't interrupt. My decision had already been made. I was going to take the plunge, brave the anger of the Negro Grandsons of Vercingetorix. At that moment I wasn't thinking about the distance we had to cover. I saw it as a straight line leading from the South of the country to the North. I was a long way from reality. I had to rely on the wisdom of Christiane, who I regarded as a sister. She showed me the route to take, the safest way to make it here, to Louboulou, before continuing on toward Pointe-Rouge.

Oweto Blues

As we fled Batalébé in the early morning, it was above all my birthplace, Oweto, that I was picturing. The figures of my parents rose up before me in my phantasmagorical confusion. Are they aware of our present situation? I don't believe so. They'll be surprised to see us appear in the North one day. We'll arrive by the main road that cuts the district in two. Our clothes will be in rags, barely covering our bodies. I'm convinced that we'll arrive in the late afternoon or evening. The entire district will applaud. We'll become local heroes, symbols of resistance, of liberty. A party will be organized for the occasion. Speeches will be made. Chief Bayo will clear his throat. I can imagine more or less what he'll say:

> Dear brothers, dear sisters, we see before us proof of courage, of endurance, and of independence. Hortense is back among us, with her daughter, both safe and sound, after a long odyssey that few among us could have undertaken in the same conditions. Some years ago, we believed in a certain idea of national unity when we agreed to a man from the South marrying our child. We were mistaken. Southerners are all alike: small-minded, deceitful, hypocritical, through and through. I'm tempted to say that it's impossible to imagine a hen living with a cockroach. As representative of the state in this district, I will henceforth be vigilant and apply to the letter the orders that come from Mapapouville. Already I rejoice that the few southerners who live in this region have been delivered into the hands of the Romans. For the rest, we know what we have to do: facilitate General Edou's task and safeguard the power of the northerners, for we were born to govern this country.

In the bush, as I walked, our bundle of possessions on my head, I imagined my mother getting deeper and deeper wrinkles since the events. Getting away from Batalébé was already a victory. The farther we went, the lighter we felt, freed of that sword of Damocles hanging over our heads. And walking, though heavy going, no longer discouraged us. My father's words kept coming back to me: "Kimbembé's a good man, like us northerners. But will he be able to stay that way among those who aren't?"

LAST PAGES
DEPARTURE FOR POINTE-ROUGE

I

〜

The Birds

The rains stopped two days ago. We've decided to leave the day
after tomorrow at dawn. On this mild afternoon the sky is clear,
but the leaves of the trees are drooping. The village is deserted;
no one is to be seen on the highway.

I can hear Mam'Soko tottering along like a praying mantis.
Her steps are getting slower and slower, and the tapping of her
cane ever more irregular.

She's at our door. She's just come in. Without interrupting my
writing, I nod to her to take a seat on the mat. She's just now
understood that we don't wish to stay here even one more day.
Her face is somber, filled with unease, as if she were wrestling
with her chronic rheumatism. Her gaze has something disqui-
eting about it. The old lady wants to say good-bye to us. But
she's pacing back and forth.

She's right behind me.

"What are you doing? You haven't been out since this morning," she says.

I reply that I'm writing. She's surprised, and she leans down
with difficulty.

"What are you writing for? Oh, I get it, it's your husband
you're writing to. Don't worry, things will sort themselves out,
marriage matters are always like that."

She's back on her feet now, and she's about to go. I ask if I can rub ash on her feet. She replies in little more than a murmur.

"There's no need, I'm fine."

She takes Maribé by the hand and disappears into the orchard. I can see them from here. They're sitting at the foot of the tree that the old lady likes to touch.

I have to organize my notebooks. Everything is in a mess around me. Torn pages. Pieces of lead from pencils I've broken while sharpening them with a knife.

* * *

Someone comes in. It's Maribé. Without looking at her, I ask what the old lady said as they sat under the tree. She hesitates for some time before coming out with it.

"She told me that it makes her very sad to see us leave. She's going to be left alone. She's gotten used to us being here. It'll be too much for her."

"Was that all?"

"Yes."

"Why did she take you all the way to the orchard if it was only for that? I'm certain she said something else to you that you're not telling me!"

"She had a bad dream last night, a very bad dream."

"What was it?"

"Birds."

"Birds? What's so special about birds?"

"They were black as can be, and they perched on the roof of the house where we're staying."

"Did she explain what that meant?"

"Yes."

"Well?"

"She said that above all else I shouldn't tell you. It might make you lose heart."

The Horizon

I've never seen so many crows crossing the sky as this evening. They're skimming over the rooftops in their funereal plumage. They take flight heavily, almost clumsily, as if they were coming out of a long hibernation. The trees in the vicinity have been invaded by these black birds. Some have landed on the ground, others on top of our house. I decide to leave my notebooks for a moment and go ask Mam'Soko about it.

Maribé stays at home.

* * *

I didn't stay long. I'm back in my corner writing these lines. The old lady seemed strange to me. I can't stop thinking about it. When I came to her door, I found it wide open. Inside, in the semidarkness I could see a thin body, half-naked, stretched out on her simple woven bed.

"Come in," she said, as if she'd been expecting me.

"The village is full of crows!" I announced as I sat on the ground next to her bed.

"I know, it's always like that."

I got straight to the point: "You told Maribé that yesterday you had a dream of black birds."

"I dreamed of those birds the day before my husband left for the other world. Of all the birds, crows are the only ones whose omens should be taken seriously. Something is about to come to Louboulou."

"What are the omens?"

"Something is going to happen. That's all I know. It's a matter of when. The crows will remain in the village up until the moment it happens. I can't tell you anything precisely. But watch out for the little one, because the way you're going to take is long, very long, and I can't see the horizon in front of you."

I left the old lady chewing her tobacco.

* * *

Night has just fallen; another day will break, our last day here. Maribé asks if I want to eat something. I'm not hungry. I'm preoccupied by the crows cawing in the darkness.

II

Among the Poor There Are Always Those
Who Are Poorer Still

I got up early, even though I'd gone to bed late last night. Mam'Soko's shadow didn't leave me all night. It seemed she was speaking to me, taking me in her arms and trying to whisper something in my ear. In my dream I heard a sentence whose meaning I still do not understand: "Among the poor, there are always those who are poorer still."

In the same dream, I believe I asked the old lady what the words signified. Then there was the cloud, the one into which she disappeared. I ran after her, but in vain. She had gotten back her legs from when she was young, and she was speeding like an arrow. I must have been thinking about her too much before I fell asleep. The dreams we have are connected with our thoughts before we go to bed, or with what we've done during the day. I keep repeating the sentence that the old lady said in the dream.

Despite everything, I want to talk to Mam'Soko, find out what those words meant.

Maribé goes with me. I take my notebook and write as we walk.

* * *

A few sheep are grazing idly in front of the old lady's house. The door is ajar. This doesn't surprise us; she always expects her husband, who comes to visit her in the night. The door has to be open so the deceased man can leave easily and go back to the other world before the living wake up. Mam'Soko must still be sleeping.

"We can come back later," Maribé says.

"No, I think she'll be up and chewing her tobacco, lying on her bed. We can go in without knocking. Come on."

The Old Lady Is Asleep

We're inside Mam'Soko's house. It's dark. We mustn't open the windows. The old lady's eyes would hurt, and she'd shout at us. She's not in the habit of getting upset, but there are some things she's inflexible about. While she's chewing her tobacco, she doesn't like to hear any noise or be disturbed by anything at all. It's at those moments that she communes with her husband, Massengo. On some days we'd come here in the morning and sit for a long time in the living room, till she was done chewing. We'd hear her, murmuring words and laughing crazily.

Today she didn't hear us come in.

We see her.

She's lying on her bed.

I cough to let her know we're there. She doesn't hear. I have to shout. To walk up and touch her softly.

We're next to the bed. Mam'Soko's eyes are open, her arms folded across her chest. Is she playing a joke?

Her jaws are clamped, with tobacco leaves between her teeth. I touch her. She doesn't respond. I move her hands and place mine on her chest.

Her heart is not beating. It stopped some time ago. We scream loudly and run out of the house. Maribé's voice carries farther than mine. The sheep that a moment ago were grazing in front of the house have bolted; they stare at us from the other side of the road, as if they'd known the news well before us.

Despite our tears and our shouts, we sense that no one is coming. So we go to the neighboring houses.

We stop at each door to give the bad news. No one is surprised. It's as if, for the local people, the old lady had been dead for years.

I look around and raise my head. There are no more crows in the trees or on our roof.

Palm Leaves

In the end a few villagers have come after all to the old lady's house. A dozen or so. Among them is one who gives the impression of being someone of note, somebody important locally. He's a stooped old man who does a lot of looking and not much talking.

"I'm the chief of Louboulou," he says as he brings his face close to the corpse, as if he were smelling it. "I'm glad for Mam'Soko, she's finally going to live with Massengo."

The other villagers stand there silently, their faces impassive. The chief of Louboulou turns toward them and gives some instructions in a language we do not understand. Some of the men run off. Finally the villagers gather outside Mam'Soko's house.

The men who ran off a few minutes ago have just placed palm leaves in front of the deceased's doorway. That's how it always is in Vietongo: palm leaves are a sign of death. When someone passes away, such leaves are put in front of their home. I don't know what it means, but it's a tradition. No one can understand it. Unless one day someone will be able to explain this practice, in which case they'll also have grasped the mystery of death.

* * *

The chief of Louboulou turns to us. He seems to be addressing me directly.

"She ought to be buried as quickly as possible; that's the custom for those rejoining a person who preceded them into the other world. Her soul shouldn't be allowed to wander for hours and hours. She could get lost. The burial will take place late this afternoon, in the little cemetery down there, close to our chief Massengo. The men will bring out the body and hand it over to the women, who'll wash her in the river. After that, Mam'Soko will be dressed in white, and she'll be able to continue her journey in peace. Do you wish to come down to the river?"

"No," I said with a shake of the head. "I don't like seeing a dead person."

Four men with fixed expressions bring out Mam'Soko's body wrapped in grimy sheets. They head off toward the river, followed by three old women whose wrap dresses trail in the dust.

The Coffin

We're back in the house. Maribé folds something in a wrap. I ask her what it is.

"Nothing," she replies.

"What are you hiding there?"

She doesn't say a word.

We stay in the house for ten minutes or so. Then we head down to the large meeting hall, in front of which the Louboulou villagers have collected.

We're there. People look at us curiously. Some of the villagers had been unaware we've been living here for two weeks.

The villagers take us for members of Mam'Soko's family. The village chief gives the order to set off for the cemetery.

We follow the locals.

One of the old women who washed Mam'Soko's body shows us the grave of Chief Massengo. It's a mound of earth with a cross on top. A few rusted lamps lie around it. There are also old shotguns, a game bag, and cartridges. The old lady is going to be buried next to her husband. The body has been brought directly from the river to the cemetery.

The coffin is a kind of crate, only loosely nailed together. The old lady must be uncomfortable inside. But what matters is the journey. In the end she'll reach her destination. We're sure of it.

The Wrap Dress and the Cane

The village chief has just spoken.

He asks if we have anything to add. I shake my head.

To my astonishment, Maribé takes a few steps forward and opens the bundle in which she had hidden something. She goes up to the open grave and throws in the walking cane that helped Mam'Soko to walk. She does the same with the wrap dress that we gave the old lady, the one she said she'd wear when she went to meet her husband Massengo.

This image brings tears to my eyes. I imagine the old lady walking alone in search of her husband.

Strong-looking men fill in the grave. Little by little, the coffin disappears, covered by earth.

* * *

We feel that the burial was a little hurried. There were songs. Hoarse old women's voices. Crows drifted across the sky without perching in the trees of Louboulou. Then palm wine was poured around Mam'Soko's grave and that of Chief Massengo, so husband and wife could raise a toast together.

One man, probably the youngest person in the village, fired three shots in the air. Those present clapped.

Everyone returned to their homes.
We felt abandoned.

The Explanation of the Dream

We're back in our house.

I'm thinking about the scene we just witnessed. On our way back from the cemetery, someone had been following us. I didn't like to look behind me.

"It's the village chief," Maribé whispered.

We stopped. He wasn't accompanied by his men. He offered me his hand as if we hadn't met before.

"Thank you for being with your grandmother right up till her last breath. The reason I'm here is because in a couple of weeks the village will proceed to the division of property belonging to the deceased and her husband. You are the only heirs, Mam'Soko told me so one time."

"No, we're not related. We're just passing through, we're leaving for Pointe-Rouge tomorrow."

The village chief looked doubtful. He was much bothered.

"Then what are we going to do about the property?" he asked with a crestfallen expression.

"What happens in this village when a dead person has no descendants?" I said without reflecting.

"Their possessions are passed on to the poorest villagers."

"Then give them to the poor."

"The problem is that these days everyone is poor here!"

"Among the poor, there are always those who are poorer still. They're the ones who can be given the property of Mam'Soko and her husband."

Among the poor, there are always those who are poorer still. The words came out of my mouth without my truly knowing where they sprang from. It was only afterward that I realized I'd heard them from Mam'Soko's mouth, in my dream.

The village chief looked at me, surprised. He'd found his solution.

He shook my hand again.

"You're a strange woman. You talk like a man, a man who has lived. Who are you? Where are you from? What are you doing here?"

"At this point it's of no importance. What matters for us is to know where we're going. And we won't know that till tomorrow."

III

A Troubled Dawn

Maribé just woke up with a start.

For a while something has been going on outside. She tries to catch my eye, but my gaze is riveted to my notebook. She checks that the door and windows are properly shut. She scurries around the whole house. I tell her to stay calm. She knows I won't budge from my corner for any reason whatsoever.

* * *

I have to finish this book; it needs to happen.

I've hardly slept at all since yesterday evening. I woke a number of times in the night with images of Mam'Soko and her hasty burial. She was smiling at me. She was coming toward me. Her cane was gone, and she had recovered from her chronic rheumatism. Her head was swathed in a sort of light. Her feet did not touch the ground. The old lady was levitating, arms spread. Behind her I could see the shade of her husband, the chief and hunter Massengo. A tall, thin, slightly stooped man. But I couldn't make out the features of his face.

In the same night, several times I touched the photograph of Christiane and Gaston. They spoke to me. At times it seemed to me that Christiane had her eyes closed and that Gaston was telling me to leave this house at once. I turned to look at the image, which I'd fastened to the wall. I was thirsty; I couldn't stop drinking. I raised the gourd over my head, and the water flowed down my chest. My forehead was streaming with sweat, as if I were climbing a mountain. I was shaking. My feet no longer supported me. So I turned around and around and bit my pencil. I checked that things were in order for our departure the next day. All was confusion inside me; it was as if I was plunged in dizziness. I heard noise, voices, footsteps. Then I went back to my corner to carry on writing this notebook. I lacked inspiration. Gaps in my memory yawned. I flipped through the pages, reread aloud what I'd just written. For the first time I'd crossed out so much that nothing was legible. I tore out those pages, then recopied them diligently. I used several candles, which burned down one after another. I knew I wouldn't be able to sleep that night, the last.

* * *

It must be about six in the morning.

This is the time we planned to leave.

The earth is moving, as if our house were about to collapse at any moment. The sound we hear outside is not the crows, even though it's coming from the sky. It's deafening. It sounds like iron clanking. Motors working in fits and starts.

I'm not mistaken: it's a helicopter that has just touched down near the entrance to Louboulou. We can also hear automobile horns on the other side of the village. Jeeps, for sure.

Maribé peeps through a chink in the window that looks out onto the main road.

"They're here! They're here!" she exclaims.

Volleys of gunfire sound close by. It's a way the Negro Grandsons have of announcing themselves. Firing in the air.

Maribé is crying.

She comes toward me. I remain impassive, my eyes still fixed on my notebook. I don't know why, but I consider it a weapon, a shield against those who are about to burst into this house.

"Mâ, they're here!"

"I know, Maribé, I know. We've lost, but I've not said my last word. They'll find me sitting down, the way they found Christiane the day after they'd committed their barbaric acts. I will not leave the house. I'm doing it for Christiane, my friend, my sister, who showed me what courage is. The time has surely come for me, but not for you. I don't see how fate could throw you to the ravenous lions. Quick, climb out the back window and hide by Mam'Soko's grave. The old lady will protect you against these fanatics, I'm telling you. Once they leave the village, walk, keep walking, and one day you'll make it to Pointe-Rouge, then Oweto. Don't worry about me. Go now."

"No, I won't leave you alone here!"

"No, Maribé! This is not the time to disobey me! You are the proof of my existence on this earth. You'll make it, but without me at your side. I'm going to give you this notebook, you'll take it with you. And you'll take the photograph of Christiane and Gaston. Behind the frame there's an important slip of paper: it's the address for Léopold Mpassi-Mpassi, who I don't know. He's Christiane's brother. At least he'll know what happened to his sister, even if he's turned his back on the country. At the first opportunity you have, send this notebook to him in France."

Scribbling My Last Words

Maribé is weeping.

I can hear war cries from relentless men. I try to scribble my last words.

Have I told everything? I don't think so. There'll always be things to add. I could spend my whole life writing our story. I really must stop.

* * *

I take the photo of Gaston and Christiane from the wall. They're sad. Perhaps they don't approve of what I'm doing. Their image is in front of me. I turn it over. There's Léopold Mpassi-Mpassi's address: Rue du Congo, 75012 Paris. I don't know Léopold Mpassi-Mpassi's house number, but Christiane, who worked for a long time in the post office, often said that the French are good at finding a residence.

I have the feeling that my notebook will make it to France and that Léopold Mpassi-Mpassi, despite what Christiane told me about him, will take the time to read it and to have many other people read it. With that in mind, I'm accompanying these pages with a general word of introduction to our country, Vietongo, in case those who read what I've written have trouble locating it on a map of the continent . . .

A Title for This Notebook

Maribé is crying more and more.

I get up. I hear footsteps in front of the house. They're here. They're trying to break down the door.

Maribé cracks open the window. She slips nimbly outside. I'm handing her the photo of Christiane and Gaston, the scrap of paper from Léopold Mpassi-Mpassi, and this notebook. I write on it the first title that comes to mind:

The Negro Grandsons of Vercingetorix . . .

ALAIN MABANCKOU is a Franco-Congolese author and Professor of French and Francophone Studies at the University of California, Los Angeles. His novels include *Blue White Red, African Psycho, Broken Glass, Memoirs of a Porcupine, Black Bazaar, Tomorrow I'll Be Twenty,* and *The Lights of Pointe-Noire.* He is the recipient of numerous literary prizes, including the Grand Prix Littéraire de l'Afrique noire, Prix Renaudot, Prix Georges Brassens, and the Grand Prix de Littérature Henri Gal from the Académie Française for his life's work.

BILL JOHNSTON'S most recent translations include Adam Mickiewicz's epic poem *Pan Tadeusz* and Julia Fiedorczuk's *Oxygen* from the Polish, as well as Jeanne Benameur's *The Child Who* from the French. He has received numerous awards for his work, including the PEN Translation Prize, the Best Translated Book Award, and the Found in Translation Prize. He teaches literary translation at Indiana University.

CPSIA information can be obtained
at www.ICGtesting.com
Printed in the USA
BVHW081012020919
557352BV00001B/205/P